*Kate has been worried about her place in Tyler's life.*

"I. . . Your love life is your business," Kate said.

"No, my love life is your business," Tyler said and strode around the desk and took Kate in his arms. "Susan has been an occasional date for community functions. That's all, and I took her out Monday night to explain that there was someone else in my life now."

"Someone else?"

"You, Kate. Aren't you in my life now?" He held her face still, mere inches from his own, and gazed into her eyes.

"Yes," she whispered and felt he had willed the admission from her. "Yes, I'm in your life."

And then he kissed her.

**VEDA BOYD JONES** writes romances "that confirm my own values," including the award-winning *Callie's Mountain*. She has also written several books in the American Adventure series for boys and girls ages 8-12 and several romantic novellas (Barbour Publishing). Besides her fiction writing, Veda has authored numerous articles for popular periodicals. A sought-after speaker at writers' conferences, Veda lives with her architect husband and three sons in the Ozarks of Missouri.

HEARTSONG PRESENTS

**Books by Veda Boyd Jones**
HP21—Gentle Persuasion
HP34—Under a Texas Sky
HP46—The Governor's Daughter
HP78—A Sign of Love
HP110—Callie's Mountain
HP154—Callie's Challenge
HP205—A Question of Balance

# A Sense of Place

*Veda Boyd Jones*

Heartsong Presents

Acknowledgment: With thanks to Pam Finley, Shari Sanders, and the crew at KSN for allowing me to watch them put the news together.

Dedication: For Landon, with love

**A note from the author:**
*I love to hear from my readers!  You may correspond with me by writing:*          **Veda Boyd Jones**
**Author Relations**
**PO Box 719**
**Uhrichsville, OH 44683**

**ISBN 1-57748-424-X**

**A SENSE OF PLACE**

*Cover illustration by Jocelyne Bouchard.*

PRINTED IN THE U.S.A.

# one

"This is Kate Malone, WKYS, reporting from the main post office in Bend, Kentucky." Kate smiled briefly at the camera she'd set on the tripod outside the building and clicked off the microphone.

"Thanks for talking to me," she told the postmaster. "This should run at ten."

As news anchor, she didn't normally film her own stories, certainly not this late in the afternoon. But today she had loaded the heavy camera, tripod, and five battery packs in the station's old hatchback and set out for the post office. Zip, her regular cameraman, had called in with the flu bug that had attacked half the station's employees over the last week.

It was a dull story. A new series of stamps featured authors from the fifties. One of the writers, Loren McFee, had been a native of Bend, but it was a slow news day, and Kate needed something else to fill the ten o'clock slot. Since the postmaster was new to the area, he didn't know much about the writer, and her interview had not been very enlightening. Kate would have to fill in the blanks after she got back to the station.

That would take a bit of research. She'd been in Bend for only six weeks herself and was still learning the ins and outs that were peculiar to every station.

Instead of dismantling the tripod, Kate filmed a panoramic shot of the half-block park across the street. Sometimes they used scenes as background for the closing credits, and this one might come in handy. She focused in on the tiny buds of a redbud tree to show that spring was in the air. As she zoomed out to encompass the tree in its setting, a sleek

Lincoln parallel parked.

A tall man climbed out of the driver's seat, shrugged out of his navy blazer, and tossed it into the car. She understood his gesture on this unusually warm day for March. But there was something more. It really wasn't his good looks and athletic build that arrested her attention. There was some undefinable power in the commanding way he tossed that jacket.

A warm breeze blew his dark hair onto his forehead, and he reached up and brushed it back. She guessed his age to be mid-thirties, and from his stance as he waited for the one-way traffic to clear, he seemed the impatient type. He hadn't noticed her, intent as he was on watching the cars so he could cross to the post office. A small boy, his dog, and a woman temporarily blocked her shot as they walked past on her side of the street.

It happened so fast, she barely kept the lens focused. One moment the dog was on his leash, and the next it had darted out into traffic. Brakes squealed. The young boy screamed, and Kate heard the thud that left the dog, a Heinz-57 variety mutt, lying at the handsome man's feet.

He knelt down and stroked the dog, murmuring words that Kate couldn't hear. The driver of the car, a teenage boy, jumped out and ran to the curb.

"It came out of nowhere," he shouted. "I didn't see it."

Three other cars stopped behind the teen's car, and traffic in the other lane halted as well, since his open car door blocked the way.

The little boy ran into the street screaming, "Woody! Woody!"

"Jacob!" the woman yelled and ran after the boy. From the woman's gray hair and gait, Kate decided she must be Jacob's grandmother.

The dog struggled in vain to get up. Jacob plopped down beside Woody and laid his head on the dog's head.

"Let's get him to the vet," the man said as he stood up.

"I didn't mean to hit him," the teen said, his arms waving madly as if he were showing the way the accident happened.

The man grasped the teen's arm. "Calm down. I know you didn't see him." He turned to the woman. "Let's get him in the backseat." He motioned with his head toward his fancy car.

"We live a few blocks away," she said and pointed south.

"I'll drive you to the vet and then back home. Jacob, can you help me lift him?"

The man knelt down and cradled the dog in his arms. Jacob held Woody's head. Through the camera lens, Kate could see blood on the animal's left side. It stained the man's white shirt, but he didn't seem to notice.

As soon as the dog was settled in the back seat with Jacob and his grandmother beside him, the man put his arm around the teen's shoulder and said something that Kate couldn't hear. The teen looked relieved, nodded, and got back in his car. The man motioned the other cars on. Then he spotted her.

He looked straight at the camera. Kate stepped aside and returned his candid stare. From across the street, she couldn't tell what color his eyes were, but they hypnotized her. Time stopped. Bells rang out. Kate knew that this was the man for her. With no logical explanation, no reason at all, she knew. This tenderhearted man with blood stains on his shirt was the one. As quickly as it came, their moment of heart-stopping awareness was over. The man shook his head and quickly climbed into his car. He turned and said something to Jacob, and then he pulled the car into the street.

As Kate watched the car speed away, the bells continued, but now she recognized the sound. It came from Community Church's belfry.

Okay, maybe the bells weren't a sign of love. But they had chimed the moment she'd looked this man in the eyes. And who could argue with bells from a church?

"Is this a sign from You?" she said with her gaze heaven-ward. The bells stopped.

She knew what they meant. Five o'clock. They rang every day at this time. She had to hurry. With practiced skill, she packed her equipment and hauled it to the hatchback.

When Kate arrived at the station, the large, low-ceilinged newsroom buzzed with its usual late afternoon chaos even though half the staff members were out with the flu.

"Did you get the stamp story?" the assignment manager asked the minute she stepped through the back door.

Tim Woolard sat at his desk, a rarity for him. Normally he paced back and forth or made calls while standing up. He was old for this job, probably in his late forties. The stress and constant tension burned most people out by that age. His brown hair was thinning on top, and he made no attempt to disguise that fact like so many TV people did. Of course, he'd never been in front of the camera. He'd been a newspaper man, had made the switch into TV ten years earlier, and loved it. He was divorced and made the newsroom his second home. Or was it his first?

"I've got the stamp story *and* a Good Samaritan story," Kate said as she unloaded the tape from the camera. "Wait until you see this. It's got all the elements our viewers love. Injured dog, the boy who loves him, a man helping out, and the accident occurred just minutes ago across from the post office. A late-breaking story."

Tim looked skeptical. He also looked ill. His eyes were mere slits in a pale face.

"Are you all right, Tim?"

"I'm okay. You like this story?"

"Trust me. Our viewers will eat this up. It's definitely more exciting than a new stamp."

"I.D.?" Tim asked and rested his head on his hand in a weary gesture.

"The boy's name is Jacob, and the dog's Woody, but I don't know the bystander who helped. I think that's okay. It gives him the anonymity of a good-deed doer. Like the mystery man who rescued survivors in that plane crash in Oregon a couple years ago. That was captured on film, and it made great footage. I'll follow this story up for the ten o'clock and get a report from the vet. Our viewers will tune in to find out the happy ending."

Okay, she didn't know which vet treated the dog, but surely she could find out before the late news.

"All right. Run with it. I'm going home."

"You're not well at all, are you? Do you need someone to drive you home?" Although Tim's workday finished at five, Kate had never known him to leave before the early news was over.

"I've felt better. I'll see you tomorrow."

Kate walked him out to his car, making sure he was capable of driving, and then she raced back into the newsroom to an editing bay and fed her tape into the machine. She cut the first part where she was admiring the man and started the clip a moment before the dog was hit. It was a good tape, focused and dramatic.

Now where should she run it? "If it bleeds, it leads" was the old newsroom adage, but the producer preferred stories that affected the viewer now. She could use it as the drop kicker, but many times the final story was cut if the newscast was heavy. That would be the producer's call.

"Kate!"

She glanced at her watch when she heard her name. The five-thirty teaser was live, and it was her turn to read the headlines.

"I'm coming," she called and labeled the tape with the banner "Dog Story." She paused in front of a mirror and grabbed her lipstick from the small shelf beside it.

"Is the copy ready?" she asked in a garbled voice as she held her lips still and applied the lipstick.

"On the desk." Mike Dodd, the producer, frowned at her and glanced purposefully at the clock behind the desk where she would read the teaser. Mike couldn't be more than a couple years older than Kate, but he'd been at the station for six years—had come straight out of college. His favorite saying, which he was fond of saying anytime there was a foul up, was "We're all communications majors, and we don't communicate."

"I'll be in the booth," he told her. The director had succumbed to the flu yesterday, so Mike was pulling double duty.

Kate had barely a minute to read over the brief copy before the cameraman held up four fingers. . .three, two, one, and jerked his hand back, her cue to begin.

"Coming up at six on your hometown news." She read the news copy, giving hints at what the sports and weather would cover, and ended with, "Join us at six for your hometown news."

The cameraman gave her the expand sign, pulling his hands away from each other as if stretching taffy, and she added, "We'll also have the touching story of a Good Samaritan helping a boy and his dog. See you at six." She smiled until the red light on the camera went off, the two seconds seeming like an hour.

"What dog story?" Mike asked.

How had he moved from the director's booth to the newsroom so fast?

"I filmed a dog getting hit and a motorist helping a little boy get the dog to the vet. I'll do a follow-up at ten."

"You want to run a dog story? What did Tim say?"

Kate glanced over at his empty chair. "He said run with it. I've got the stamp story for ten. I'll edit it after supper."

"All right. Bring me the dog story."

She retrieved her tape, hurried to the director's booth, and handed Mike the edited version.

"Any graphics?" Mike asked. Normally the major players in a video were identified with a cut line across the bottom of the screen.

"None. No I.D., but I should have some by ten," Kate said.

"Slow news, but let's not lead with this. How about fourth?" He slipped the tape into a slot and wrote the number and the length of the video on his master list.

Kate left the small booth which housed twenty-some seven-inch TVs. Every time she was in the director's booth, she was glad she wasn't in the high-tech world of counting seconds and pushing specific buttons. A director could break or make a newscast by bringing up the wrong video or losing the sound. Mike seemed jumpy, and she attributed that to the stress of doing both his job of producing and taking on the sick director's job.

Of course, she was pulling double duty, too. Although she still did reports for series news stories, regular reporting wasn't her normal routine, but that was how she'd begun her broadcast career. Fresh out of college, she'd been a reporter at a small station in Iowa. From there she'd gone to Rochester, Minnesota, as a noon anchor. Soon she'd been promoted to weekend anchor, then to weekday evening anchor.

She'd applied for the anchor job in Bend because it was a bigger TV market. This job was the next rung on the ladder and had the bonus of being fairly close to her family. Located by a bend in the Ohio River, the city was right across the water from Indiana, her home state.

Kate walked back to the newsroom and asked reporter Debra Bowman to call around to vets until she found the one working on Jacob's dog.

"When you find him, see if we can get film."

Kate typed the dog story in capital letters in the computer.

Since the players in the drama weren't wearing microphones, she hadn't captured their words, so she had to explain a bit to the viewer. That finished, she printed out the story on the multi-copy form and tore the pages apart.

She distributed the different colored sheets to several places in the newsroom and took a copy to Mike in the booth.

For the next few minutes, Kate read aloud her pink copy of the other news stories. A few feet away John Yeager, the male anchor, was reading his blue copy out loud. He was an old timer at the station, having been there for sixteen years. He'd told Kate that during that time he'd had six female anchors. She was the seventh. The women had moved on to bigger cities and bigger markets, but John was content to stay in the area. He had kids in school, and his wife taught English at the local college. This was home to him, and he intended to stay put. He'd been kind to Kate, offering help whenever she needed it.

The noise in the studio changed tone. A low, tension-edged murmur of voices filled the space.

"Ready?" John asked. He stood, adjusting his tie in front of the long mirror beside the sliding glass door to the studio.

Kate slipped into a navy-blue blazer and straightened the lace collar of her blouse. She added blush and more lipstick and then followed John into the studio.

The concrete-floored room was huge, and each corner held a different set. The main news desk had swivel chairs for four. The newly named Storm Center had multiple TVs that looked important, although they had nothing to do with the old-fashioned radar tracking system that was connected to one computer. An old dot-matrix printer sat on one shelf. It wasn't even hooked up, but the viewer couldn't tell that and probably thought it was a Teletype machine, receiving up-to-the-minute reports form the National Weather Bureau. TV was an image, not a reality. The empty green screen for rear projecting of weather maps hung beside the Storm Center.

The kitchen corner held cabinets and a cooking island that allowed preparation whenever the noon "Sandy Moore Show" featured a cooking guest. The final corner was the interview set—couch and chairs that Sandy Moore used for her community interviews and the crew for *This Morning* used for the early news show.

Kate shivered when she sat down in her chair, not from nerves, but from the sixty-two degree temperature in the studio. The equipment needed to be cool. Once the bright lights were turned on for the newscast, the place heated up fast.

Okay, maybe nerves caused a couple shivers. Fifty miles away, her folks, her grandparents, and probably her youngest sister, in Sulphur Springs, Indiana, sat in front of their TVs waiting to see her. Sometime in the newscast she touched her hand to her heart, the signal that said "I love you" to her family. That was one of the perks of being at a station the size of WKYS. Its powerful signal reached a large rural area that wasn't serviced by cable companies.

Camera one was focused on her, and she watched the familiar finger countdown.

"Good evening. And welcome to WKYS with your hometown news. I'm Kate Malone." She looked into the camera instead of at the computer prompter directly below it that scrolled the words she was to read.

"And I'm John Yeager. At the top of our news. . ."

❧

Tyler Sinclair paced the waiting area of the veterinarian's office. This was not the way he'd intended to spend his evening. He'd left early from his top floor office at the Sinclair Corporation to run a few personal errands, and then he'd witnessed Jacob's dog getting hit. He'd never met the boy, but there was no way he could leave an injured animal on the street with that little boy crying over him. The boy's grandmother had called her husband. When he arrived, then maybe Tyler could leave.

"Do you think he'll be all right?" Jacob asked for the hundredth time. The boy sat by his grandmother. Tyler knew Jacob had been close to tears several times, but the worried little boy had held them back.

"He's with a good doctor. They'll do the best they can for him," Tyler said.

What was taking so long? He'd called the vet from his cell phone and caught him before he'd left his animal hospital for the day, so he'd seen Woody as soon as they'd unloaded him.

The poor mutt. He must be doing all right. So far the vet hadn't called Jacob back to make the dreaded decision about having Woody put out of his misery. Tyler swallowed hard. He'd had to make that decision when he was eleven, except his dog was ill with leukemia. He remembered that day as if it were yesterday, and he wouldn't wish it on anyone. He'd never gotten another dog. The pain of losing Lucky had been too great to bear again.

"You think he'll be all right?" Jacob asked once more. "God won't let him die, will He?"

How could he answer that?

"God watches over everything," Jacob's grandmother said. "He keeps His eye on the sparrow, so I think he has His eye on Woody, too."

A good answer, Tyler decided. He didn't know how it would go with the dog. A broken leg was evident by looking at him, but he could have internal injuries, too. The cut on Woody's side had bled a lot but hadn't looked too deep.

Tyler glanced at his watch. Almost six o'clock. The corner TV was silent, but he reached over and flicked it on. Good, it was tuned to his station and not a competitor's. Well, actually it was the family station, but as CEO of Sinclair Corporation, which held several diverse companies including WKYS-TV, he referred to it as his own.

He'd been at the helm for only six months now. Each month he had scrutinized a separate company, familiarizing himself with the key personnel and statistical reports. This month he had focused on a trucking firm. He had even gone on a three-day haul with a driver so he'd understand the types of problems his employees ran into. He'd scheduled WKYS for June.

His method of management might be unorthodox, but that was how he'd always operated in the air force, and so far that style had worked for him. He'd made major at a young age, but he'd never forgotten what it was like to be a second lieutenant. He didn't ask his men to do something that he'd not be willing to do himself. Nor did he sit behind a desk making decisions. He'd flown with his men, aware of each training maneuver for pilots, and he made it his business to know what kept a plane in the air. He knew the crew chiefs who maintained the planes, and he knew the sizes of engines.

The news anchors flashed on the screen. Kate Malone was the woman he'd seen across the street. Of course, he'd watched her on the news before, but it had taken him an instant to recognize her when he saw her in front of the post office. She hadn't looked like the same in-charge woman who read the news. She'd seemed vulnerable, more feminine. She'd been wearing a mid-calf-length floral skirt and a frilly white blouse. In his mind's eye he could see her as she had been that one instant this afternoon.

He studied the TV screen without listening to the news. She still wore the white blouse, but the lacy collar was all that could be seen. The rest was hidden by a severe navy-blue blazer with the station logo on the breast pocket. He might have to recommend that the anchors not wear uniforms when June came and he spent some time at the TV station.

Movement down the hall shifted Tyler's attention, and he

saw the vet stroll toward them.

Jacob yelled, "Look!" Tyler turned toward him. The boy's eyes had doubled in size, and he was pointing at the TV.

Tyler looked at the screen in time to see himself watching the traffic, and then Woody bound into the path of the car.

"There's me!" Jacob shouted.

"The Good Samaritan took Woody and Jacob to the vet," Kate Malone was saying. "We'll have an updated report on the condition of the dog on the news at ten."

Tyler stood hypnotized, staring at the set. In the distance he heard a phone ringing and ringing in the office before some-one finally picked it up.

"Telephone for Jacob," the veterinarian's assistant called out. Tyler surmised that something must have happened so that Jacob's grandpa couldn't come yet. He heard Jacob say he'd wait at the vet's office.

Tyler turned back to the TV in time to see the station had gone to a commercial break. Kate Malone. Kate Malone. She had filmed the whole thing. He was her mystery Good Samaritan. He hoped his eccentric grandmother wasn't watching this. She shunned publicity, and as the ruling matri-arch, she demanded that the entire Sinclair family stay out of the limelight.

Since Tyler had come back to town, he'd upset her more than once when his picture had been in the newspaper. Because the Sinclairs owned the TV station, publicity on TV had never been a problem. Until now. Tonight he was the guess-who-our-mystery-guest-is celebrity. In his mind, he rearranged his schedule. He'd tackle WKYS in April, not June.

Jacob tugged on his arm.

"I'm going to be on TV," he said. "The TV station is com-ing to interview me. You, too, Mr. Sinclair."

"This should be good publicity," the vet said. "Thank God the dog's going to be fine."

"Grandpa," Jacob shouted and ran toward an older man who had just opened the outside door. "We're going to be on TV."

"Not me," Tyler muttered to himself. He turned to Jacob's grandmother. "Now that you have things under control, I must be going. An appointment."

"A TV reporter is coming," she said. "Couldn't you stay for the interview?"

"Afraid not," he said and smiled tightly.

"Thanks so much for your help. I don't know what we would have done without you."

"You're welcome." He squatted down and patted Jacob on the shoulder. "Take care of Woody."

"I will. I promise."

"Goodnight," Tyler said and strode outside to his car.

❧

"What do you mean that was Sinclair?" Kate asked. When she'd finished the report on the dog accident, she'd expected her co-anchor to ad lib about the kindness of strangers. Instead John had sat spellbound, staring at the monitor. As soon as they'd gone to a commercial, he'd turned on her.

"What have you done? That was Tyler Sinclair of *the Sinclairs*. They own this city, and that includes this station. Heads will roll over this."

Did he mean her head? "But why? I showed him in a good light."

"That doesn't matter. It's their unwritten policy—no publicity. When Vince Sinclair died, the family wouldn't let us put it on the air. When Tyler came back to take over the corporation after his brother's death, he wouldn't give us an interview."

"But how was I—" She stopped as the cameraman's fingers counted down.

She smiled at the camera and introduced the weatherman's segment in the Storm Center corner of the studio. Their mikes were probably still live, so she didn't say another word to John, instead studying the stories on her pink sheets. Her head pounded. She couldn't believe that she had committed such a faux pas. With forced professionalism she pushed the event to the back of her mind to deal with after the newscast. She read the rest of the news, smiled at the camera, gave ad-libs when expected, and collapsed as soon as the all-clear sign was given at six-thirty.

Tim burst into the studio. Why was he back? He still looked ill, but adrenaline had to be carrying him. "Why didn't you tell me that Tyler Sinclair was your Good Samaritan?" He turned to Mike, who had followed him into the studio. "I'd never have let her run with this story," he said, "if I'd only known. I got back here as fast as I could for damage control."

"Not your fault," Mike said. "You didn't assign her the story."

Oh, great. They were both looking at her as if she had lost her mind. *Dear God, help me out of this mess*, she prayed.

"I didn't know who he was," she said, her hands palms-up in a gesture of defeat. "If the Good Samaritan had been John Doe on the street, would you have liked the story?"

"We don't want to hear logic now," Mike said, as he slid the glass door to the side and led the way back into the newsroom. "I want to know defense. I'm the producer, and he'll attack me first."

"Isn't 'attack' a little strong?" Kate asked.

"Hard to say. It's really old Mrs. Sinclair we have to worry about. His grandmother's a bit strange," Mike said.

"Strange?"

"Weird. Odd. Eccentric," Mike elaborated. "Don't worry. We'll handle this. You couldn't have known how that family is about publicity."

Two reporters were talking on phones. Chelsea Cooper, Kate's closest friend at the office, hung up and made a tally mark on the dry-marker board. "Response on the dog story is strong," she said. "Eighteen calls so far wanting to know the outcome—which is broken leg and bruises and scrapes. Debra should be at the vet's office by now. She found the right one on the third call."

"Good," Kate said.

"Any calls from the Sinclair family?" Mike demanded.

"No," Chelsea answered as the phone rang again and she picked up the receiver. "WKYS newsroom." Her eyes widened, and she stared at Kate. "One moment," she said into the receiver and punched hold. "Make that one call from the Sinclair family," she corrected herself. "And he wants to speak to Kate."

# two

He had debated calling. He'd even read the framed Proverb that hung on the wall behind his desk. "A quick-tempered man does foolish things. . . ."

His mother had given it to him after he had graduated from college and had then joined the air force without consulting the family. At that time he'd had it with the family trying to run his life. His decision to join the service wasn't the result of a quick temper but more of a slow burn.

He'd argued with himself about talking to the news anchor, but at the end of the three-minute debate and after listening to messages from his mother and grandmother on his answering machine, he'd looked up the number of the station and dialed it.

"Good evening, Mr. Sinclair. Kate Malone here." From her tone, he could tell she was all business and probably already knew that she had violated a directive of the Sinclair family.

"Miss Malone, is it your journalistic practice to film people without their knowledge and to use that film on the six o'clock news?"

"It's my journalistic practice to film news as I see it. The piece was quite innocuous. And I did present you in a good light, Mr. Sinclair."

She had him there. Even his mom had admitted that, but she still didn't want a Sinclair on the news. It was Grandmother he was worried about. The slightest publicity stirred her up, and it took days to settle her down again.

"Will you show the footage again at ten?" he asked in a cool voice.

"Not if you request that I don't. I didn't know your identity before. Now I do."

That stopped him. She hadn't known who he was. He'd tried to keep a low public profile, but whenever he attended a charitable function, the press managed to get him in a random shot and run it in the paper. In the back of his mind something clicked, and he remembered that she was a fairly new anchor. When he'd returned to Bend, a blond had been the female anchor. Kate Malone had cinnamon-brown hair. He closed his eyes and could picture it blowing in the breeze that afternoon.

"However," she continued after a short pause, "we'll be running an interview with the boy and we'll tell our listeners the extent of the dog's injuries. We promised that on the six o'clock, and we have a reporter at the vet's office now."

"Yes, I know, but leave me out of it."

"Certainly, Mr. Sinclair. Oh, we've had countless phone calls already asking about the condition of the dog. And several viewers have commented on your act of kindness. Perhaps the story has given Sinclair Corporation and its new CEO a public relations boost."

"Thank you, Miss Malone." Tyler hung up the receiver. Kate Malone seemed to have all the answers, but a news story featuring a family member was not how Sinclair Corporation used publicity. The corporate publicity department singled out members of its companies for recognition. The Bend *Gazette*'s Thursday business section had a least one Sinclair story in it, complete with a picture of the employee who'd been promoted or attended a conference or received an honor.

But publicity had not always been good. Two weeks ago the paper had run a front-page story on economic development with the focus on the need for diversity. Although the article covered small area towns outside of Bend and each town's major industry, some reporter had cleverly targeted

Tyler's corporation in the headline: "If Sinclair sneezes, Bend gets pneumonia." The article had dealt mainly with the twenty-six percent unemployment rate found in nearby Willow when a corporation that employed twenty-two hundred people had moved out of that town of eleven thousand. Bend's population was eight times that, but Sinclair did own several industries in the city.

Tyler couldn't argue with the logic of economic diversity. Sinclair Corporation was built on diversity so that a bad year in one company wouldn't cripple the corporation. The newspaper failed to mention that Sinclair owned some companies outside Bend and even outside Kentucky. The never-the-complete-story type of journalism was one reason the family frowned on publicity.

Another reason was to give the family privacy. They were the wealthiest family in Bend, and their lives had been the focus of rumor and speculation. Since his grandmother had always been a bit strange about publicity, the family had bowed to her wishes. She had told Tyler when he was a young boy that their family in Bend was watched as much as the royal family in England, so he should always behave.

Tyler reached for the phone after the second ring. He'd considered letting the machine pick it up but knew he'd have to answer to his grandmother at some point, so he might as well get it over with.

The voice on the other end was not feminine.

"Were you coming to see me when you became the famous rescuer?" Joel asked.

Tyler's good friend from high school worked at the post office, and when Tyler returned to town he'd renewed the friendship. Joel was a breath of fresh air. He didn't care that Tyler was a Sinclair, and he didn't care that he wasn't in Tyler's regular social circle, which was made primarily of business contacts. Joel just seemed glad to play racquetball with

Tyler, and Tyler knew he could be himself around his friend.

"So now I know you watch WKYS at six," Tyler said.

"Are you kidding? They have the best-looking anchors. I liked the blond one before this one, but there's something about Kate Malone that's special. It's in her eyes."

Tyler would have to agree, but he didn't say that out loud.

"Did you give her a piece of your mind over this story?" Joel asked. "She came in the post office, and I met her before she did the interview with the postmaster. She's something. It's definitely in the eyes."

"I've spoken with her," Tyler admitted. "She didn't know who I was or she wouldn't have run the story."

Joel howled with laughter. "That did the old ego some good. Is your grandmother off her rocker over this one?"

"A tad disturbed. But I made sure Kate Malone won't run that story again at ten," Tyler said.

"You didn't upset her, did you?" Joel sounded as if he were Kate Malone's personal protector.

"Let's just say she now knows who owns the station."

"What about that dog? Was it hurt bad?"

"Broken leg. It'll be all right. She'll run an update on the dog, but she'll leave me out of it."

"Well, you tell her she can interview me anytime she wants," Joel said, and Tyler could hear his friend's grin through the phone line.

"I was coming to see you about playing racquetball tonight, but in all the confusion I forgot. Got time for a game?" Tyler could use some physical action right now.

"And a bite to eat afterward? I'm starved."

They arranged to meet fifteen minutes later. Tyler threw his gear in a sports bag and was walking toward the door of his apartment when the phone rang. He let the machine pick it up, since he again expected it to be his grandmother. He didn't have time to get into a lengthy conversation with her.

This time it was a feminine voice on the machine, but not an elderly one.

"I saw you on the news, Tyler. They called you a Good Samaritan. This is a side of you I've never seen before."

Susan Appleby.

"I was wondering when we could. . ."

Tyler locked the door behind him, effectively shutting out her voice.

&

"What did he say?" Mike demanded when Kate hung up the phone, which immediately rang again. Chelsea picked up the receiver. "Since I'm producer, I'm surprised he didn't chew on me."

"He merely asked me not to run the clip again. You heard my side. I told him we'd do a follow-up, but leave him out of it."

"That's it?" Mike asked, shaking his head. "There are bound to be repercussions. Not that I blame you, Kate. You couldn't have known."

"What's the big deal?" Kate asked. "Do the Sinclairs have something to hide? Why do they shun publicity?"

Mike shrugged. "It's been the policy since before I started here." He sounded as if that was enough of an explanation.

"Well, now that I know it, I'll abide by it," Kate said and was relieved when he nodded and let it go at that.

"Anyone going to eat?" John asked. As a rule the other anchor, the weatherman, and the sportscaster went out together, and on rare occasions they asked her. Although he offered the general invitation, John was looking at the other men, so Kate took the hint. Probably they wanted to discuss her big goof anyway.

Chelsea put down the phone again. "I'm leaving before this rings one more time. It's given me a headache. Are you going to supper?"

"I'm going a little later," Kate said. "First I want to get this stamp story edited so I don't go down to the wire again." She didn't know how she could possibly mess up a story on a 1950s writer, but she would have it ready for Mike to see before she took her dinner break. She wouldn't give the producer another reason to be upset.

She was upset herself. She'd misjudged Sinclair. She hadn't even met the man, but that look they had exchanged that afternoon was not something she could easily dismiss. She had thought he was the one—as if all she had to do was find out his name, meet him again, and they would live happily ever after. Fairytale land, that's where her mind had gone. As if one brief moment could change her life forever. But it had been such a strong feeling.

*Forget it,* she told herself. *Forget him, and get to work.*

She fed Loren McFee's name into the computer that was hooked up to the Internet, then waded through a list of his books with reviews before she came to a brief biography of the writer.

She gasped. Loren McFee had been murdered in Bend, Kentucky, on May 1, 1959. His killer had never been arrested. Her curiosity, which made her such a strong reporter, was piqued.

Here was another name to add to her series on unsolved murders. With sweeps month coming up in May, when TV stations competed for a share of the viewing audience in the ratings, Tim had given her the assignment to cover notorious murders where the killers were still at large. Bend was fairly quiet in the murder department for a city of 85,000, and she hadn't thought of digging this far in the past to find victims, but a writer famous enough to have a stamp in his honor would certainly find a place in her series.

She reached for the spiral notebook she had started on the subject, added pertinent facts on Loren McFee, and made a mental note to get a couple of his novels from the library.

Perhaps some of the McFee family still lived in the area, but the phone book revealed no McFees. Well, she could start with the local paper's coverage and perhaps turn up some names there. Certainly the trail of a killer would be cold after forty years, but there had to be some of the victim's friends left in the area. People were usually very forthcoming when they could talk to the camera about someone famous they had known as a friend.

That series was going to be a winner, but for right now she focused on completing the story on the stamp's release, with only a reference to the murder and a mention of the other three writers whose likenesses were also on the new stamps.

Kate had finished typing the story into the computer when the back door opened and Debra Bowman stumbled in with a camera case in one hand and a tripod in the other.

"Got it," she said triumphantly. "That kid was a natural. A boy and his dog. It's corny, but it works." She headed for the equipment room, then appeared at the doorway a moment later with a tape in her hand. "I'll edit this. Shall we do a live newsroom shot? Where's Mike?"

"He went to dinner with John and the others," Kate said and didn't comment on the newsroom shot.

Debra would not be content to be a reporter and noon anchor for long. A true camera hog, she suggested a live interview shot with her on every story she brought in. She buddied up with Mike and Tim whenever possible, probably thinking that the better friends she was with them, the better stories she'd be assigned.

"I'm headed to supper myself," Kate said. "Be back."

The men were on the parking lot, returning from their dinner break, when Kate walked outside. She told Mike that her stamp story was on his desk. Chelsea pulled in and parked her compact in the spot next to Kate's two-year-old Olds. She climbed slowly out and held up her hand in greeting.

"Maybe tomorrow night we can go out for a bite instead of tonight's rush," Kate said.

"Yeah, sure," Chelsea said. Her voice lacked her normal cheerfulness.

"Are you all right?" Kate asked.

"Can't shake this headache," Chelsea said. "I'll take some more aspirin. See you later."

Kate settled behind the wheel and pulled into the street. She liked Chelsea. She wasn't the stab-you-in-the back-type like Debra. It hadn't taken Kate one week on the job to have every staff member categorized. There were the same types in every station.

The get-ahead-at-any-cost types like Debra Bowman were easy to spot. The career meant everything, and Debra was aiming for a number one market—New York. WKYS was ranked 82 in market size, so Debra had a long way to go. She'd probably aim for Louisville or Tulsa next.

Bend might be a good spot for Kate, but she hadn't decided that yet. She liked the city. It was the perfect size—big enough for lots to do and small enough to maintain a neighborly quality—and she liked the proximity to her family in Indiana. But six weeks in the place wasn't enough time to make a decision to never send her video tape sample out to another station. Debra sent out three resumes and tapes a week, aiming upwards, always upwards.

Maybe John Yeager was right, and Bend was the place to settle down. She'd keep an open mind about that and trust God to lead her to make the right decision. In the last few months, she'd been discontent, and she wasn't sure why. She hoped her ambition was properly focused. Did she want to go farther and farther into broadcast journalism, or did she want a more traditional life with a husband and a family? Choosing one over the other wouldn't make her more successful, but she needed to know which one would make her happy. For now she was inclined to stay put. That is, if she still had a job after affronting Tyler Sinclair.

Kate made the turn into the library parking lot and spent a few minutes picking through McFee's novels. There were nine on the shelves, and she decided to start with the one with the earliest publication date. Didn't most writers put some of themselves into their books, particularly in their early works? She checked out two books, then headed to the barbecue place a few blocks east of the library. She didn't indulge herself with her favorite food very often, but after an evening as stressful as this one, she deserved a treat.

Shorty's Barbecue on Main Street was little more than a hole in the wall halfway down a block. If all tables were full, which they were most of the time, the restaurant held forty people at most. Tonight the place was packed. With no parking lot nearby, the street was lined with cars parallel parked. Kate pulled in a block away and walked back to Shorty's. She intended to get her sandwich to go, so she maneuvered around customers waiting for a seat and stepped to the cash register.

She quickly ordered and paid for her food and got a takeout number, then stepped back. The familiar feeling of being watched slid over her, and she turned toward the dining room.

Even though she'd been at the station for only a few weeks, she was already recognized when she went out in public. She viewed it as one of the benefits or drawbacks of the job, depending on the type of day she was having.

A young girl, holding out a pen and paper napkin, approached her.

"Can I have your autograph?" she asked and glanced back toward a table where two adults and a couple boys sat watching. "I've seen you on the news. My name's Kate, too."

Kate took the pen and napkin. "Did your brothers dare you to ask me?"

The young girl nodded. "How'd you know?"

"I've got a couple brothers, too," Kate said. She signed the napkin, With best wishes from one Kate to another, Kate Malone. "Here you go. Have a good evening, Kate."

The girl scurried back to the table and handed the napkin to one of her brothers.

That watched feeling still bothered Kate, and she glanced around the place again. Observing her from across the dining room was Tyler Sinclair. She opened her mouth and closed it without uttering a word. She didn't know what to say, even if he could have heard her over the din of so many voices. It was one thing to talk to him on the phone, quite another to see him in person. She didn't smile; she didn't frown. She merely stood, blocking the way of the next take-out customer. She was as mesmerized this time as she had been this afternoon. For a long moment they maintained eye contact, then he glanced at his companion and said something.

The man sitting across the table from him looked familiar. Oh, yes, she'd spoken with him briefly that afternoon at the post office. Both men stood, but Tyler Sinclair shook his head and the man sat back down, leaving Tyler to walk toward her alone.

Time took on a slow-motion quality as she watched him approach. He stretched out his arm, and she reached for his hand. He held onto her hand and put his other hand on her shoulder and led her back to his table. It was almost as if he didn't think she would follow him if he let go.

The other man stood once more. She couldn't remember his name, and if there was one thing she excelled at, it was names. James. . Joe. . .

"Kate, you remember Joel Jamison," Tyler said, taking her off the hook and finally letting go of her hand. She extended it to Joel.

"Of course," she said and shook his hand. "You were kind enough to get the postmaster for me today." She hadn't planned to sit down, but the two men were obviously going to remain standing until she did, so she sat in the chair that Tyler had pulled out for her.

"How did your interview go?" Joel asked.

"Very well, thanks. It will air at ten."

"Along with a follow-up on the dog story," Joel said and winked at her. "Don't let this guy get to you." He nodded at Tyler. "His bark is worst than his bite." He laughed, and Kate smiled at his little dog joke.

She looked at Tyler, who was watching her, and resisted the urge to smooth her hair.

"We didn't get off to a very good start," she said. "I apologize again for putting you on the air without your permission."

"It's all right. I'm aware that you're new here, and you didn't know there are some people who prefer not to be in the spotlight."

"True, I'm new, but that doesn't mean I'm not going to go after any story that is newsworthy."

She didn't know why she made that statement. It must seem to him that she was out to antagonize him, and that wasn't the case. She wanted him to know that she wasn't easily intimidated, and she thought the way she had let him lead her to his table hadn't given that impression. "Oh, I know that a dog story isn't earth shattering, but if there were a story about the Sinclair Corporation, I'm sure you wouldn't want our station to ignore it. You wouldn't censor the news, would you?" From the look in his eyes, she seemed to be making the situation worse instead of better.

"There is such a thing as freedom of the press," she continued. "And the right of the public to be informed."

"I wouldn't argue with the First Amendment. But I have an argument with irresponsible TV journalists who get one side of a story or interview someone and then give quotes out of context, which distorts the facts," he stated as if he'd been the victim of such an interview.

"Surely you're not accusing me—" Kate pointed a finger at him, then pointed it at herself.

"No. I'm merely stating that the Sinclairs prefer to remain out of the news."

"You may not grant an interview, but you wouldn't censor the news, would you?" she asked again. She couldn't seem to keep herself from pushing the issue.

"Who has the pork?" the waitress interrupted.

"Right here," Joel answered.

She placed a homemade roll piled high with thinly sliced pork in front of him. "Beef?" she asked before she set the other sandwich down for Tyler. "How about you?" she asked Kate.

"I have a takeout." She held up her number.

The waitress looked at it. "I'll check on it," she said and headed toward the kitchen pass-through window.

"Listen, if you ever need to interview somebody, you can call on me," Joel said.

"Thanks," Kate said and smiled at him. She turned to Tyler. "But I can't interview you," she said.

"No," Tyler said and hesitated a moment before he added, "It's a family directive. If there's a change of policy, I'll let you know." He reached for the barbecue sauce and spread it liberally on his sandwich. "Kate Malone, you're right. We have gotten off to a rocky start, and I'd like to change that."

"Me, too," she said and waited for him to tell her exactly how he'd do that.

"Here's your sandwich." The waitress picked up Kate's number tag from the table and left a white paper bag in its place.

"Well." Kate stood and picked up her sack. Tyler immediately stood, too, and Joel put down the barbecue sauce and jumped to his feet.

"I've got to get back to work. I'll see you later," she said and moved toward the door.

"Good to see you, Kate," Joel said.

She looked back and waved.

"I'll call you," she thought she heard Tyler say, but she was too far away to be sure. At the door, she turned for a last look and again felt that magnetic pull as he stared at her.

Outside she took a deep breath of March air that had turned cold now that the sun had set. She huddled into her blazer and hurried to her car, chastising herself all the way back to the station for the things she had said to Tyler Sinclair.

What a fool she had been. They could have had a civil conversation, but she had to make a stand for freedom of the press. Why couldn't she keep her mouth shut? Why couldn't she have talked about the dog story or the weather?

Joel seemed like a nice guy. He was personable and funny. Why couldn't she feel that same spark toward him that she felt when she looked at Tyler?

Tyler Sinclair. He vacillated between being cool one minute and warm the next. Did he really say he'd call her or was that wishful thinking? And why would she want that anyway? Hadn't she already decided she had misjudged her initial reaction to him?

At the station Kate sought out Chelsea to tell her about meeting Sinclair, but one look at her friend, stopped her.

"My headache has escalated to a full-blown body ache."

"Get out of here," Kate said. "Go home."

"I'm supposed to get an interview at the hospital about how many flu patients they've had. Mike wants to lead with it tomorrow morning."

"You'll be a patient there if you don't get home and lie down. I'll do the hospital story."

"I already have the school superintendent with statistics on how many kids are missing school. The two interviews have to go together."

"I'll take care of it," Kate said. "Now get out of here, and don't breathe on anyone else. I'll check on you tomorrow."

After Chelsea left, Kate viewed the tape that Debra had edited. She had to admit that the reporter had coaxed real emotion out of Jacob. The vet had given standard replies to easy questions about the dog's condition, but Jacob's words of love for his dog tugged at heart strings. So, maybe this wasn't the stuff that made big headlines. It was what made WKYS a hometown news station. When she'd interviewed for this job, the station manager had told her they were trying to change the station's image from big city with the symphony and Minor League baseball team to small town with friendly neighbors at the park. Hometown news. That was the new slogan, and Kate liked it.

The rest of the evening, she went over stories for the ten o'clock broadcast. Most were updates on what they'd presented at six, but a new slant was needed so that the news wasn't just a rerun of what they'd read before.

Although she answered the phone several times and gave updates on Woody's condition when the calls were inquiries from dog lovers, that special call didn't come in. She really didn't expect him to call at the station, did she?

Her home phone was unlisted. She'd learned that was important at her previous job in Rochester. She'd gotten tons of calls from nuts. One woman complained that Kate had enticed her husband away from her. Instead of eating supper at the table with her, he ate in front of the TV so he could watch Kate!

No, if Tyler didn't call her at work, he wouldn't be able to reach her.

Ten o'clock came. She introduced the dog story tape, then the camera went to the live shot in the newsroom where Debra gave a current update. There was a glitch at the end of the news when Mike cued up the wrong tape, but otherwise it went all right.

At ten-thirty Kate said goodnight to the viewing audience, smiled at the camera until the red light went off, then headed out to film Chelsea's assignment. He hadn't called.

## *three*

Tyler unlocked the front door of his old brick house and ushered Joel inside. He'd bought the place shortly after he'd returned to Bend. As soon as he'd discovered that the old Massey home was on the market, he'd snapped it up.

In his childhood he'd been fascinated by all the nooks and crannies of the place whenever he went with Brian Massey to visit his old uncle. The round brick columns that held up the second floor verandah gave the place a masculine touch of strength and class that matched the character of the old gentleman who had lived there.

The place needed rewiring, central heat and air, and a new roof, but the large brick home showed not one sign of settlement problems. There were no tale-tell cracked brick joints. The house was as solid as the day the first of three generations of Masseys had moved in.

While the renovations were being done, Tyler had stayed with his mother and grandmother in the big family house on the hill overlooking the city, and he'd moved into the Massey house only a few weeks earlier. It already seemed like home.

"The game's already started," Tyler said, "but we can catch most of it." He led Joel through the large entry to the den and clicked on the giant television.

"This place always amazes me," Joel said. "Surround sound, big screen. We're almost on the court with these guys." He settled into one of the large stuffed chairs that faced the television. Tyler settled into one beside it.

"One thing about a house this big, there's room for everything," he said. There were several rooms upstairs that had nothing in them. He'd claimed the master bedroom and out-fitted one room for guests but left the others unfurnished for now.

At time out, Tyler headed to the kitchen to get them each a soft drink. The light blinking on his answering machine caught his attention as he passed by his office. Three blinks. One call was from Susan Appleby, the call he'd heard earlier as he was walking out the back door. With a sigh he strode to his desk and pushed the button. He listened to Susan's throaty voice, then his grandmother's voice demanding that he call her and explain about the dog. The final call was an apology from the TV news producer, Mike Dodd. He explained that Kate Malone had not known the unwritten policy that the Sinclairs were not news, and he assured Tyler that it wouldn't happen again.

That call wasn't necessary. Kate Malone didn't need any-one to apologize for her. His opinion from watching the news the last few weeks was supported by their brief meeting at Shorty's. Kate was a strong woman who did what she thought was right and would defend her decisions.

The producer's call would have been better directed toward Grandmother. She must be upset since she'd called again and left a second message. At least his mom hadn't called again. Tyler should call them, but he'd wait until after the game and the late news. When Grandmother saw the follow-up didn't rerun the tape of him, maybe she'd simmer down.

She could get worked up over the smallest thing. He'd been visiting in Bend three years ago when the new library had been dedicated. Grandmother had discovered that a reading room had been named after some deceased author, and she'd hit the roof. She'd felt the room could have been named after a dozen local people who had contributed more than that writer.

Tyler remembered how she'd stormed around the family

home, slamming doors, and then she'd settled down. To his knowledge, she'd never set foot in the library again, and he knew she'd marked the library off her list of charitable contributions.

He liked his grandmother. She'd been there for him count-less times when his dad and mom made what he considered unreasonable demands on him in his youth. But she could sometimes be unreasonable, too. Yes, his best defense in this dog publicity situation was to let her calm down, then he'd talk to her.

Tyler walked into the large kitchen and grabbed a couple Cokes from the refrigerator.

"Game's back," Joel called from the den.

"I'm on my way," Tyler said.

The game went long and at ten o'clock was tied with five minutes to go. The score had see-sawed back and forth, and fans couldn't have asked for more exciting entertainment.

"Do you mind if we change to the news?" Tyler asked.

Joel looked at him as if he were out of his mind.

"We can switch back at commercial," Tyler added.

"Oh, the dog story. Okay."

Tyler immediately switched channels and watched the lead-in where the news anchors were introduced. Kate was pictured in her office wearing a forest green suit with her hair brushing her shoulders; on location by a creek, wearing jeans and a red sweater with her hair in a ponytail; in a pants suit, sitting in front of a group of school children; in a black evening gown at the symphony, interviewing the governor; and finally at the news desk in her station blazer.

Joel was right—it was in her eyes. They looked at a man in such a soft way. Even at Shorty's when she had defended her right to report the news and those blue eyes had been flash-ing, they were still kind. He had the feeling that she would not intentionally hurt another person. Concern, that's what was in those eyes. She cared about people.

"Good, it's their first story," Joel said.

Tyler concentrated on the television. A reporter told what had happened earlier without rerunning the accident tape. She talked with the vet and then Jacob. The boy's story was touching, and he thanked Tyler for helping save his dog. In a live interview in the newsroom, the same reporter gave an update, saying the dog was still doing well and a full recovery was expected.

"That wasn't bad," Joel said. "You were barely mentioned, and just by the kid."

"Yes, that was fine. Want to see the rest of the game?" Tyler offered, although he would rather watch Kate.

"Wait. There's my boss."

Kate's afternoon interview with the postmaster was on, and although her voice was heard, the camera stayed focused on the man, who held up a sheet of stamps. Tyler remembered how she had looked in the frilly blouse and flowery skirt and wished she'd been on the air in that feminine outfit.

"Okay, you can switch it. I can tell the boss I saw his interview, but now let's catch the end of the game."

The camera was on the other anchor, John Yeager. That guy had been around a long time. Tyler first remembered seeing him when he'd been home on college breaks and every time after that. He clicked back to the basketball game, and they watched the final tense minutes. As soon as it was over, Tyler switched to WKYS.

The sports segment was already on, but as soon as it was over, Kate appeared back on the screen.

"For those of you who joined us late, we'll repeat that the dog Woody, whose accident was shown on our six o'clock news, is doing fine. His broken leg has been set, and his scrapes and cuts bandaged. Thank you for your calls about the little fellow."

"We've had more calls about that dog than any other recent story," John Yeager said. "Here again is Jacob, the dog's owner."

The video that came up was the accident scene with Tyler bending over the dog. Five seconds of the tape ran before it was cut and the camera focused on the startled news anchor for a moment before switching to the film of the reporter interviewing Jacob.

"They messed up," Joel said. "Going to call them?"

"No. Someone obviously got the wrong tape, but he realized it soon enough."

"Are you going to call Kate, like you told her?"

"I shouldn't have said that. Maybe she didn't hear me. It was pretty loud in there," Tyler said, but he thought she'd heard him.

"She heard you. I could tell by the way she tilted her head. She's interested in you. It was in her eyes."

"You keep saying that. You have a thing about her eyes?"

"They're such a pure blue," Joel said.

"I know. I'll bet those eyes are one reason she's a news anchor. Not that she isn't good. She is."

"So, are you going to call her?"

"I'll probably call her," Tyler said, but he didn't know, and he didn't want to confide to Joel that he was afraid she might turn him down. That thought made him feel like a high school boy, and he was the CEO of a multi-company corporation. The uncertainty he felt didn't match his corporate image.

He was just as afraid that she might feel obligated to see him because he was her boss. Hadn't Joel felt obligated to watch the postmaster's interview? But Kate didn't report to him on a daily basis, and that was a big difference. Still, sexual harassment cases were common these days, and he didn't want to give a hint of impropriety.

"There she is." Joel focused on the television.

"And that's the news. Remember tomorrow at six the entire news team will be on location at Southpark Mall's Women's Fair. Join us then. Good night."

"I might have to go out to that Women's Fair if you don't call her," Joel said.

"What is this, an ultimatum? If I don't pursue her, you will?"

"I wish. She didn't look at me like she looked at you. Give her a call. Hey, I'm out of here," Joel said.

Tyler walked him to the door. "Want another chance to beat me over the weekend?"

"Sure. Just give me a call," Joel said.

Tyler shut the front door and locked it. Now what should he do about Kate Malone? Most people who worked nights didn't go home and straight to bed, did they? Didn't they need time to unwind after a work day, just like those who ended the day after an eight-to-five job?

In his office, he looked up her phone number but didn't find it. Of course, she'd been there only a short while and wouldn't be in the phone book. He dialed directory assistance. He'd get the number before he made a decision about calling her. When he made business decisions, he liked having all pertinent information at his fingertips. It was the same in his personal life.

The operator told him her number was unlisted. That problem was easily enough circumvented. He dialed WKYS and asked for Mike Dodd. The producer came quickly to the phone.

"I'm glad you called," Mike said. "I've been trying to reach you and getting the busy signal."

"Yes, well, I'm after Kate Malone's home phone number. Or is she still there?" That possibility hadn't dawned on him until just then.

"No, she's off on assignment, but the error on the ten o'clock was totally mine, not hers. Our director's out with the flu, and I was running the booth. I had two tapes labeled 'dog story,' and I pushed the wrong button. I can't believe it happened, and I'm really sorry."

"That's okay. I understand. What about Kate's phone number?" Tyler put his pen to paper, waiting for the numbers.

"But she's not responsible for that tape being run again. I am."

"It's okay, Dodd. I'm not going to reprimand her; I just want to talk to her."

"You just want to talk to her?"

"Yes. May I have her phone number?"

"It's unlisted."

"I'm aware of that. Could you give it to me, please?" Getting her number was harder than he'd thought possible. First Joel had defended her, now Mike Dodd. Were all males this protective of Kate?

"Could I have her call you?" Dodd asked. "I don't like to give out her number without her permission. She's rather paranoid about it."

"Fine," Tyler said in a brusquer voice than he intended. He gave his unlisted number to Dodd, who promised he would immediately page Kate.

"Thank you," Tyler said after Dodd had apologized once more.

Now he had to wait for the phone to ring. If she returned the call. If she answered her page immediately.

The phone rang, and he grabbed it.

"Hello," he answered.

"Tyler, she's had a heart attack." Even though her tone was taut and higher pitched than normal, he recognized his mother's voice.

"Grandmother?"

"Yes. She's had a heart attack or a stroke or something. She just collapsed."

"Where are you?"

"I'm in the car following the ambulance out the driveway. They're taking her to Mount Carmel."

"I'm on my way." He grabbed a jacket from the hall tree and dashed out of the house.

"Dear God, let her be all right," he prayed over and over.

His cell phone rang as he pulled out onto the street.

"Yes?"

"I just wanted to make sure you were on your way," his mother said.

"I'll be there in five minutes," Tyler said. He gunned the car, aware that he was speeding, but the empty streets didn't make it a hazard. He wanted to get there by the time the ambulance arrived. He was closer to the hospital than the Sinclair mansion on the hill, but the ambulance would have speed on its side.

He should have called Grandmother back after her first call, before he'd gone to play racquetball with Joel, and certainly when he'd returned home and found her second message. Why'd she get so worked up over this? Would his picture on the news cause her to collapse? Could simple stress cause a stroke? Surely there was a medical reason. He wouldn't feel unnecessary guilt over this, he told himself, but it settled on his shoulders anyway.

He heard the siren before he saw the flashing lights of the ambulance ahead of him and followed his mother's car into the hospital parking lot. He parked beside her and jumped out and opened her door.

"Tyler," she said with a sob and hugged him. "She just collapsed."

"Let's not panic until we know her condition." He escorted her to the emergency room door, and they stood to the side and watched as his grandmother was unloaded from the ambulance.

She looked dead. Her skin was grayish, and her eyes were closed. An IV was threaded into her thin arm.

"How is she?" Tyler asked the attendant.

"Holding on. We'll know more after some tests. Doctor will talk to you later." He wheeled the stretcher through the emergency reception area, around a corner, then through automatic double doors that closed behind him, blocking Tyler's view of the emergency room cubicles.

He answered questions from the emergency room staff and filled out a few forms with his mother's help.

"Let's take a seat, Mother." What else was there to do but wait? There were only a handful of people in the waiting room, and they were all sitting together. He guided his mother to an isolated area off to the side where he had a view of the door through which his grandmother had been taken. "How did this happen?"

"She was watching the news. She was upset about you being on there, you know. Why didn't you call us back?"

Tyler explained that he'd been out for the evening. "Joel and I watched the basketball game, and I was going to call after the news."

He glanced up when he heard the sound of the automatic doors on the emergency room opening. He expected to see a doctor coming to report on his grandmother's condition. Instead, Kate Malone appeared, carrying a large case and a tripod.

"Kate?" He immediately walked over to her.

"Oh," she exclaimed. "What's wrong? What are you doing here?" She set the heavy case down.

"My grandmother's been brought in. What are you doing here?"

"I just filmed an interview on the flu epidemic and the number of cases out here. How's your grandmother? What's wrong with her?"

"We're uncertain right now. She collapsed. Could be a heart attack."

"I'm sorry. Is there anything I can do to help?"

"No. It's a waiting game now."

She nodded and glanced behind Tyler where a distraught-looking woman sat. She was obviously his mother. The resemblance was there in the dark hair and the eyes. "Well, I'm sorry," she said again. She picked up the heavy case and walked around the corner toward the exterior entrance.

Her pager had gone off while she was interviewing an emergency room doctor, but she had ignored it once she saw it was the station number. If she drove back to the station without calling first, then she'd have to return if something more was needed from the hospital, so she pulled her cell phone out of her purse.

The master control person answered and called Mike Dodd to the phone.

"I'm finished at the hospital. Is there something else you need here?" Kate asked him.

"No. You had a call from Tyler Sinclair. His number is 555-4892. He wanted your home phone number, but I didn't give it to him. I figured you could call him and give it to him if you wanted. He said he just wanted to talk to you. I made it clear that it wasn't your fault that a few seconds of that dog tape ran."

"I'll talk to him," Kate said. She quickly wrote down his number in case she'd ever need it.

A moment ago Tyler hadn't said anything about having called her at the station. Of course, he was obviously upset about his grandmother's condition. Kate could walk back and visit with him while he waited, but he didn't need a continued discussion about freedom of the press. And if his call had been more personal, which she doubted, now wasn't the time to get to know one another. What he needed was a close friend to talk to.

What about Joel?

She found a pay phone with a directory, looked up his number, and then glanced at her watch. It was after eleven, but wouldn't he want to know? Although she tried to be a logical mind-ruling-heart type of person, when it came down to emotional decisions, she always relied on the Golden Rule.

How would she want to be treated? If her grandmother had been taken to the emergency room with a heart attack, she would want her best friend to be there with her, lending support. And Joel seemed like a good friend to Tyler. Joel had teased about Tyler's bark being worse than his bite. He wouldn't say that in front of a casual acquaintance, would he?

With no more hesitation, she dialed his number. The phone rang just once before he picked it up.

"Joel, this is Kate Malone."

"Kate?" Surprise was in his voice.

"I'm sorry to call so late, but Tyler's grandmother is at the hospital with a possible heart attack. His mother looks pretty upset, and I thought Tyler might need a friend with him." Maybe this hadn't been such a good idea. Maybe men didn't support each other the way women did.

"Are you there?"

"Yes. I was filming a story."

"I don't do very well at hospitals. Is his grandmother bad?"

"I don't know. He said she collapsed."

"Okay. Would you meet me outside and go in with me?"

"Sure," she said. What was wrong with Joel? How could he not do well at hospitals? There was nothing to do but sit with Tyler. "I'll watch for you and meet you outside the emergency room door."

"All right. That's a good plan. Which hospital? Mount Carmel?"

"Yes."

"See you in ten minutes."

Kate carried her equipment out to the hatchback that had WKYS painted on it in big letters and loaded it. She looked around the well-lit parking lot and found Tyler's Lincoln before she walked back to the entrance.

She couldn't blame Joel for not liking hospitals. They were places of death, but they were also places of hope. Medical science had come a long way in finding cures for illnesses, but sometimes they went too far. Sometimes they kept people alive when their quality of life was gone. How much better to let them go on to their spiritual reward.

She didn't know the facts in this case. She didn't know how old Tyler's grandmother was or what had caused her to collapse. All she could do was pray that God's will for Tyler's grandmother would be something Tyler could deal with.

Kate watched several cars drive in the lot and park and finally saw Joel climb out of one of them. She crossed the driveway to meet him.

"I'm glad you're here," he said. "I guess we should go find out how she's doing." He sounded reluctant to go in, and he reached for her hand and held it tightly as they walked to the emergency entrance. The automatic doors slid quietly open, and Kate breathed the antiseptic smell of the hospital again.

Joel's grasp on her hand tightened, and she looked up at him. His skin was pale under the fluorescent lights.

"He's right around this corner," she said.

When Tyler saw them, his eyes widened, and he rose to his feet. His mother stood, too.

"Joel?" she exclaimed.

"Are you all right?" Tyler asked Joel.

"I'm fine," Joel said, but he quickly sat down in the chair next to Tyler's.

"How did you know I was here?"

"Kate called me. She thought you might need a friend, so I came. How's your grandmother?"

"We're not sure. Still waiting for the doctor to come out."

He turned to his mother. "This is Kate Malone. Kate meet Alma Sinclair."

Alma nodded to her, and Kate murmured, "Nice to meet you."

"Joel, would you like some water?" Alma asked.

"No, I'm all right. Just took a minute for me to get my bearings." His color was coming back. While Alma talked to him, Kate looked at Tyler, silently asking for an explanation. He moved over beside her.

"Joel hasn't been in a hospital since his dad was killed in an explosion out at the munitions plant," he said softly. "He was nine at the time. How did you convince him to come?"

"I said you might need him." Her respect for Joel soared. His willingness to go to the hospital told her how much he valued Tyler's friendship.

"He's a good friend," Tyler said. "Thanks for calling him."

"Sure. I, uh, got the message to call you."

"Yes, I had hoped we could talk—"

"Mr. Sinclair." A doctor had come up behind them, and Tyler turned around.

"How is she?" he asked.

"She's stable. We're moving her to intensive care, but tomorrow we'll know more about her condition. I believe she's had a mild stroke on her right side. She's conscious now, but her speech is garbled. It's too early to tell, but I'm hopeful that with physical therapy she'll be able to talk again and return to a fairly normal life."

"What caused this, doctor?" Alma asked.

"It was probably an arrhythmia. A sudden change in blood pressure can cause a blood clot to turn loose from an artery lining and rush to the brain."

"Could stress have caused this? Could something that upset her cause her blood pressure to surge?" Alma asked.

He pursed his lips as if in thought and then said, "It could."

## four

"A video of Tyler Sinclair saving a dog couldn't have make her have a stroke," Mike told Kate once she arrived back at the station.

"Tell that to the Sinclairs," she said. "You ought to have seen the way Alma Sinclair looked at me." With mechanical movements, Kate stowed the camera in the equipment room and put the batteries in place to be recharged. Guilt rested on her shoulders, and she didn't understand why it weighed so heavy. She agreed with Mike that a flattering story about Tyler Sinclair, where he wasn't even identified, could not have brought on a stroke.

"Where's the video Chelsea did on flu in the school?" she asked.

Mike retrieved it from the pile on his desk. "I appreciate your working late. That flu story should be our lead tomorrow on *This Morning*. I told Tim I'd have it ready."

Kate nodded and took the video along with the one she'd just shot at the hospital and headed to an editing booth. The flu bug had hit the schools as hard as it had hit the station. This story at the front of the morning news show would reassure parents that their kids were not alone suffering from the ailment. Some schools across the river in Indiana had shut down for a couple days to curb the epidemic. She wondered if it would get that severe here in Bend. Once she finished combining the two videos, Kate typed the lead and left everything on Tim's desk.

It was after midnight when she pulled into the drive of her duplex. For a moment she sat in the car, weariness creeping over her. Then she picked up the McFee books and her purse and went inside her sterile apartment.

She'd been here six weeks, and she still hadn't hung pictures on the white walls. Unpacked boxes sat in the spare bedroom that she intended to use as an office. Only the small kitchen was totally unpacked and homey looking. A painted wooden tray her grandmother had given her leaned against the wall above one counter, and colorful hot pad holders hung on another wall beside the built-in oven. Ceramic canisters with butterflies on them sat beside the toaster that her mother had given her when she'd moved into her first apartment.

Not unpacking was unlike her. She'd call herself a nester, and in the past she'd unpacked quickly and made each place a home. In Iowa she'd found an old farmhouse on the edge of town and redecorated it, painting and wallpapering, even though it was a rental. In Minnesota, she'd located a century-old carriage house beside a mansion and turned it into a unique home. Both moves had been heart-wrenching. But this time she'd sensed the transient nature of her job and had not rushed to make a home a hard place to leave.

Maybe Debra's undisguised shoving to reach another rung of the ladder of success was rubbing off on her. No, she wouldn't put herself in Debra's class. Kate had just been too busy learning the ropes of the new station and attending public events to gain the recognition that was a necessary part of her job. On three of her six weekends in Bend, she'd driven the fifty miles to see her family.

Unlike her other residences, this one lacked character, so she justified her reluctance to decorate it as a waste of time. Maybe in the back of her mind, she admitted, there was the notion that if it was a home, she'd have to leave it, and if it was just a place to sleep at night, she would stay put. That was ridiculous, she knew, but something prevented her from putting her stamp on this duplex.

As weary as she was, she couldn't fall asleep. Thoughts of Tyler Sinclair took over her mind. Eight hours ago she hadn't met the man; now she'd seen him three times. When she'd first laid eyes on him, she knew he was the one for her. Well, that was a laugh. Her woman's intuition was on the blink. It hadn't told her that he was her boss or that she shouldn't interfere in his family's life or it would have big consequences— like his grandmother having a stroke. Not her fault, she told herself for the hundredth time. Not her fault.

"Dear God," she prayed, as was her nighttime custom, "if it was my fault, I'm sorry. Forgive me. It wasn't intentional. Please help Tyler's family live with whatever is Your will for his grandmother."

She didn't know what else to say. Surely it was coincidental that Mrs. Sinclair had had a stroke tonight. It was absurd to think there was a connection. There was nothing to that story—it was fluff. Boy and his dog. An innocent incident had been blown way out of proportion.

To take her mind off the Sinclairs, Kate reached for Loren McFee's first novel. It chronicled small-town life in the South. From the first few pages, she'd label him a readable Faulkner. His style was not so rambling, but he captured characters with a few well-crafted sentences as competently as Faulkner. She got so caught up with the story of a small-town lawyer, that she read for an hour before turning off her bedside lamp.

The ringing phone woke her. She glanced at the sunlight streaming in the east windows and then at the clock radio. Eight-thirty.

"Hi," Chelsea said as soon as Kate answered. "I thought I'd catch you before you brought me chicken soup. I'm well."

"You don't have the flu?" Kate shook her head to dislodge sleep and concentrate on what Chelsea was saying.

"Nope. Just a sick headache, I guess. Thanks for taking care of that interview last night. I owe you one."

"And I'd like to collect," Kate said. She explained the events at the hospital.

"So, what do you want me to do?" Chelsea asked.

"Since you're from Bend, you must know Mrs. Sinclair."

"I only know *of* her. We've never met. But my great-aunt Betsy knows her."

"Could you call the hospital and find out how she is. I'm persona non grata with the Sinclairs."

"I'll see what I can find out," Chelsea said.

Kate had already showered and dressed in jeans and a sweater by the time Chelsea called back.

"Still in intensive care, but that's all I could weasel out of them," she said. "You're not responsible, you know."

"I know," Kate said, although she wasn't entirely convinced.

"What you need is to get out for awhile and do something new and exciting. Have you had breakfast?"

"Not yet."

"Good. I'll pick you up in ten minutes, and we'll go to a place that has the best omelets in the world."

It did no good for Kate to protest. Besides, she probably needed a dose of Chelsea's brand of cheerfulness.

Within half an hour, they were seated at the counter of Mary Lee's, an old-fashioned café that could have come out of Loren McFee's novel. On the opposite wall of the long narrow room were booths covered in red vinyl. All were full with what appeared to be regulars from the senior set. Kate watched a waitress place fresh baked lemon meringue pie in the glass-fronted pie safe on the back wall.

"Is it against the law to have lemon meringue pie in the morning?" she asked.

"I think it's mandatory here. How can they make meringue that high?" Chelsea said and dug into her omelet the second the waitress set it in front of her. "That headache made me ravenous."

As soon as they had both polished off their eggs and pieces of pie, they climbed back in Chelsea's car. "Hope you don't mind a couple of errands since we're downtown."

"I'm just along for the ride," Kate said and contentedly looked out at the downtown buildings.

Chelsea paid a couple utility bills, then pulled up in front of the post office. "Uh-oh, the scene of the dog crime," she said. "I'll just be a minute."

"No, I'll go in with you," Kate said. This was even better than having Chelsea call the hospital. Joel could tell her how Mrs. Sinclair was and what had transpired after she left last night.

He wasn't at the window where he had been yesterday, so Kate asked about him, and a woman called to the back. A few moments later he came to the counter.

"Kate, I'm so glad to see you," he said. "I appreciate you making me go to the hospital last night."

"I didn't make you," she said.

"Yes, you did. You asked me, and how could I turn down a gal with such pretty eyes—especially since you had Tyler's interests at heart."

"How's his grandmother?"

"Holding her own. After Tyler and his mom saw her in intensive care, they went home for a few hours, but they're back out there this morning. Tyler called a few minutes ago to say she'll be moved to a private room later today."

Kate looked down at her hands. "Do they still blame me?" she asked in a low voice.

"That's crazy. They couldn't blame you. Alma was just upset last night or she'd never have insinuated that a TV story could cause a stroke."

"I know," Kate said.

"Ready?" Chelsea was at her elbow.

"Okay." Kate turned to leave but noticed Joel casting an

interested eye at her friend. She introduced them and watched with awe as sparks flew between them. "Thanks for the information, Joel." She turned with a wave and dragged Chelsea outside with her.

"Wow! Who is that guy?" Chelsea said breathlessly.

"He's a friend of Tyler Sinclair's. What's with you two? I've never seen anything like that, unless. . ." She remembered the afternoon before when she'd first seen Tyler and been drawn instantly to him. "Oh."

"Yes, oh!" Chelsea seconded. "I need to get my phone number to him. What do you think? Should I drop him a postcard?" She laughed at her little joke.

"I imagine he'll find you," Kate said. "Give him a chance."

Chelsea pumped Kate for every drop of information she knew about Joel, which was quite a bit, considering she'd just met him the day before. And her intuition was working again, because Joel took his chance to find out more about Chelsea that evening at the news remote location at the mall.

Kate had ridden with the remote operator in the old van, since his helper was out with the flu. Mike thought it a good idea that she learn all aspects of her new job, which included carrying chairs and a make-shift desk to an area near the food court in the mall. The remote man would also serve as cameraman on this shoot. John Yeager and the sportscaster and weatherman would be on location by five-thirty to test microphones and bring the last of the news copy.

Kate dodged people as she carried chairs through the throng who packed the mall for the Women's Fair. From flower shops, hospitals, wedding boutiques, and travel agents to diet food suppliers, the abused women's shelter, and civic clubs, all were represented in a multitude of six-by-six-foot booths that ran down the center of the wide mall walkways.

After Kate had toted folding furniture, she watched the remote operator put up the forty-foot mast on the van and helped tape down cables that ran to their makeshift desk and the camera. Via her cell phone, she called Mike at the station to make sure someone would be running the computer prompter. With him still doing double duty as director and producer, that was one detail that could slip by everyone, and one that would stop the news cold. There was no foot pedal on location for Kate to run her own copy.

With all connections ready, Kate read the five-thirty teaser from a piece of paper she'd taped below the lens of the camera. A crowd gathered around to watch her, even though it was just a thirty-second spot.

Kate sat alone behind the cardboard desk and read over her copy, taking time to speak to passersby whenever they spoke to her. In the bystanders waiting to watch a live broadcast was a man she'd seen before. Where was it? Oh, yes, here at the mall during the home show. That location shot was the first one she'd done in Bend. She remembered the man because he'd stared only at her, never looking at the others. She felt his eagle-eyed stare again and glanced up with as pleasant a smile as she could muster. There was something unsettling about him. He was average height and weight, hair thinning a bit on top, but he probably wasn't over thirty. He smiled back, and she relaxed a bit.

Since she'd only seen him at the mall, that was probably where he hung out, and she was letting her imagination work overtime to think there was something strange about him. She was a little gun-shy since her experience in Rochester with a stalker. That man never did smile at her. He merely watched her every move. Whether she was at the grocery store or the laundry, he'd be there. At every location shot, he'd be there. When the calls started, she'd had the police investigate, and sure enough, he was their man. She'd changed her number, and the man was ordered to stay away from her. He never threatened harm, but he'd made her nervous enough that she was still more aware of people wherever she went.

She glanced up again at the odd man and saw that he held a broom and a long-handled dust pan. He worked at the mall! No wonder she'd seen him here on the last location shot. He was just looking for more excitement than he found pushing a broom around the food court.

She breathed a sigh of relief and glanced at her watch. The minutes were ticking by, and where was the rest of the news team? By a quarter till six she was getting nervous that John Yeager and the others still hadn't arrived.

"They're stuck in traffic," Mike told her when she answered her cell phone. "Some kind of wreck. Debra and Chelsea are there now and will get them to the mall. They should be there by weather time if not before. Don't explain it. John will give details when they arrive."

Kate swallowed hard. Okay. She'd done the news alone before, but she hadn't done the weather and the sports. And not with a live audience gaping at her. The crowd gathering around was swelling as the clock ticked closer to six.

She reread her copy and what she had of John's. Instead of a reference set on her desk, she'd have to read his straight off the prompter and hope whoever was running it kept it moving right along.

The cameraman held up his hand and counted down his fingers. Five, four, three, two, one. . .

"Good evening. I'm Kate Malone, and welcome to your hometown news coming to you live from Southpark Mall's Women's Fair. At the top of our news. . ." She read the news copy and smiled at the camera. At the first commercial break, she glanced at the crowd, and her attention was drawn to the waving arm of Joel Jamison. She smiled at him, and her gaze travel to the group of Girl Scouts to his left, who were also waving.

She should have known Joel would show up here. He

couldn't know that Chelsea wouldn't be on a location shot. If she had a report airing, her introduction segment would come from the newsroom.

After the news, she'd give him Chelsea's phone number if he asked. She glanced back at him, and her wide smile froze on her face. Standing next to him with his arms folded over his chest was Tyler Sinclair. He wasn't smiling, but he wasn't frowning either. He stared at her, and she stared back, their gazes locked.

The cameraman said, "We're coming back," and held up his hand.

Kate smiled at the camera and read more news copy. While a taped report was airing, John Yeager slid into the chair beside her.

"I'm so glad to see you," Kate whispered.

"Stuck in traffic," John muttered as he clamped his mike onto his station blazer. "A truck full of rats, mice, and rabbits jackknifed."

"Full of what?" Kate asked.

"Laboratory animals. Some were killed, but some high-tailed it out of those broken crates. Guess they got a reprieve for life. Road's still closed. Had to have Debra come get us from the other direction and leave Chelsea with the station wagon. What a mess. We're lucky to be here now."

Kate looked at the camera. "Joining me now is the rest of the WKYS news team. John, I understand you've had quite an adventure."

John explained about the jackknifed truck and then gave a lead-in to the weather. While the camera was on the weather-man, Kate stared at the big-screen TV that was showing what the viewer at home could see—weather maps, current temperatures, and eventually the forecast. She could feel Tyler's gaze on her, but she didn't acknowledge it.

Why was he here? Joel must have brought him along.

"Looks like spring is in the air," John was saying to Kate. She was expected to ad-lib something back, as if they were sitting at a dinner table, but she couldn't think of a thing to say that didn't involve Tyler Sinclair.

"We should enjoy it before that next front moves in bringing heavy rain," the sports broadcaster said. "If it hits before Sunday night, it could ruin Deer Hollow Golf Tournament's final day. We'll find out who finished on top today, right after these messages."

Through this interruption, Kate listened to an in-depth report on the wreck from the weatherman, who said he'd seen it coming when that truck had passed them half a mile before the accident. Kate looked at him the entire time he was speaking, and then from under her lashes glanced toward Joel and Tyler as she turned back toward John.

Debra was chatting with them! She had the most ridiculous, simpering look on her face. And they were smiling back, especially Tyler, who was now saying something that caused Debra to laugh. Joel looked up and caught Kate's eye and shrugged as if he didn't know what was going on. Kate looked down at her copy. They were coming to the end of the sports segment. Time for a recap and a closing. Then what would happen? She focused on the moment, read the material, and smiled at the camera.

"We'll be back at the station for the late news. Before then, why not come out to Southpark Mall and visit the wonderful booths? We'll see you again at ten."

"We're clear," the cameraman said. The big-screen TV showed the beginning of the six-thirty sitcom rerun.

"What a deal," John said as he took off his mike. "I knew you could handle it here without me, but I figured you wouldn't want to do weather and sports."

"You've got that right," Kate said.

"Well, I guess we can help you pack this stuff up," John

said. "Maybe by then Chelsea will be here with the station wagon. We were cramped in Debra's hatchback."

"Here, I'll help with that," Joel said. He took the folding chair out of Kate's hands. "Where's your friend? She works at the station, doesn't she?"

Kate glanced at the crowd that was milling around now that the news was over. She didn't see Tyler or Debra.

"Yes. Chelsea works at the station. She'll be here pretty soon, but she doesn't normally go out on remotes." She scanned the crowd again, and then she picked up her purse and another chair and led Joel toward the exit where the van was parked.

"Hey, you'll put in a good word for me with Chelsea, won't you, Kate?"

She laughed. "Sure I will. Can I tell her that you like her?"

Now he laughed. "I do sound pretty immature, don't I? Why don't you give me her phone number, and I'll do the rest."

"Good plan," Kate said. They put the chairs in the van and started back into the mall. She pulled her ever-present notebook out of her purse and jotted down Chelsea's name and number.

"Why don't you add yours in case I need to get hold of you sometime?"

Why not? She didn't give out her number to many people, but she really liked Joel. His easy-going way reminded her of her brother. She wrote her name and number down, too.

"I'm in the book," he said, "any time you need a friend."

"I know. I called you last night."

He nodded. "Who's that gal annoying Tyler?"

Now that the crowd had thinned, Kate easily followed Joel's line of sight. "Debra Bowman. A reporter. How do you know she's annoying him? He looks to me like he's enjoying her company." She hadn't meant to sound so catty and wished she could take back her words.

"Nah. He just didn't want to be rude to her. Let's rescue him."

Joel took her arm and steered her toward Tyler or she would have gone back to the portable set to finish dismantling it. The other members of the news team were still chatting with a few people from the audience and didn't seem concerned with getting the work done and getting back to the station. Actually part of their on-location broadcast duty was to shmooze with the crowd. Only the remote operator was carrying equipment toward the exit.

"Tyler, look who I found," Joel said.

Tyler looked relieved to see them and turned their way even though Debra was still speaking.

"Kate, I've been wanting to talk to you about last night." The way he said it made her think something actually went on between them besides his mother practically accusing her of causing his grandmother's stroke.

"I'm sorry I didn't call you back," Kate said. "It didn't seem like the right time." Let Debra interpret that any way she wanted, and from the look on her face, she seemed to have read into it exactly what Tyler wanted. He looked smug. She looked miffed.

"Excuse me," he said to Debra and took Kate's arm and led her off to the side. "Sorry. But I had to get rid of her."

"How's your grandmother?" Kate asked.

"She's out of intensive care. A mild stroke. With time, she should recover. Kate, your dog story didn't cause it. My grandmother is a stronger person than that. She has her idiosyncrasies, and she'd dead set against publicity, but she's not irrational. I'm explaining this badly. You'd have to know my grandmother. She sticks to what she thinks is right, but she doesn't invent problems that aren't there."

"I'm glad you feel I'm not to blame. Does your mother share that opinion today?"

"Of course. She was upset last night and grasping for anything that would explain it."

"Kate!" She heard her name being called, and both she and Tyler turned toward the sound. "Coming with us?" John Yeager looked at her companion and said, "Never mind."

"I'd better get back to work," Kate said.

"Kate!" This time it was Chelsea who came flying toward her. She stopped short when she saw Tyler and then her mouth flew open when she saw Joel talking with Debra. She did a quick about turn and walked over to the news team.

"I'd better go," Kate said. "I'm on your time clock, you know." She watched Joel leave Debra standing alone and make his way to where Chelsea stood. "Your friend has a crush on my friend."

"So it seems."

"Kate!" The remote operator was ready to go. All the equipment had been loaded.

"That's my ride. Goodnight, Tyler. I'm glad your grandmother's doing better." She walked away, aware of Tyler's gaze on her.

# *five*

"Well, I got mine," Joel said. A wide grin split his face as he drove Tyler back to the hospital. "Chelsea's going to dinner and a movie with me tomorrow night. What about Kate? Did you make your move?"

Tyler squirmed in the front seat. He felt as if they were back in high school again, plotting how to ask girls out.

"No, the opportunity didn't come up."

"You can call her at the station," Joel said.

"I shouldn't," he answered. "In a big sense, I'm her boss. I don't want to make her uncomfortable, make her feel forced to go out with me."

Joel laughed. "She wants to go. You didn't see the look on her face when she saw you with that reporter. She's interested, all right. Call her." He turned into the hospital and drove up to the front entrance.

"I guess I'll have to ring her at the station. I still don't have her home number."

"I have it," Joel said. "What'll you give me for it?"

"She gave you her number? Why?" Tyler felt a frown line settle on his forehead. He didn't want to be envious of his best friend, but why did he know so much about Kate Malone? And why did they have such an easy-going relationship that she'd give him her phone number?

"Don't worry, buddy," Joel said and reached into his shirt pocked for the page out of Kate's notepad. "She and I are friends, and I think she'll be a very good one. She's dependable."

"How do you know that?" Tyler didn't want Joel telling

him about Kate's attributes. He wanted to discover them on his own, but that would take talking to her for more than three minutes at a time.

"Instinct. . .and Chelsea trusts her. They're good friends. Kate was at the hospital last night on Chelsea's assignment because Chelsea didn't feel well. Kate helps her friends. She called me to come sit with you in the waiting room because that's what she would do in the same situation. You have to learn to read women, Tyler."

If there was one thing Tyler didn't need, it was for Joel to lecture him on women. Sure, Joel had two sisters who were constantly fixing him up and telling him how to relate to females, but Tyler had never been at a loss for dates.

Even in the air force, when fraternization with noncommissioned officers was forbidden—and that eliminated most of the women he met on post—there were plenty in nearby towns who were eager to go out with an officer. There had been a few daughters of older officers, but that could be a road to disaster, Tyler had learned quickly.

Since he'd been back in Bend, there had been no shortage of women wanting to date the new head of Sinclair Corporation, but he had grown tired of being pursued just because he had a powerful position and a fat wallet. Susan Appleby came to mind, and he blanked her out. Tyler would rather be the pursuer, and Kate Malone was worthy prey.

"You getting out?" Joel asked. "There's a car behind us."

"Oh, sorry. Lost in thought. Could I have that number?" He pulled a small organizer from the inside pocket of his sports coat and jotted down her number as Joel read it out loud.

"Want Chelsea's, too?" Joel asked.

"That's okay. I'll stick with this one," Tyler said. "Thanks for coming by to see Grandmother."

"Sure. I'll check with you later," Joel said and pulled away as soon as Tyler climbed out of the car.

Tyler stood under the covered entrance to the hospital and took a deep breath of March air. It wasn't as warm as it had been yesterday, but that spring-is-here smell of freshly turned dirt and new growth in the carefully tended hospital flower beds made him smile. Spring was a new beginning, and he felt a rebirth in himself.

With his grandmother in the hospital, he should feel uneasy and upset. But he felt hope inside, something he hadn't felt in a long time. Kate Malone had brought him that euphoric feeling. Just being near her set his heart pounding and adrenaline flowing. For too long now he'd felt nothing but stress and the loneliness of decision making. Losing his father, losing his brother, resigning from the air force, and taking over the family business—all had taken their toll on his sense of humor and his outlook on life. He'd been struggling to find a sense of place in this new life of his, and finally it was taking shape.

He wanted to get on with living, and interest in Kate Malone had forced him out of his private melancholy. It wasn't that he hadn't dated since he'd returned to Bend, but his dates all had the forced brightness of a first date—chatter, not feelings. With Kate there were feelings. He wanted to know all about her, and he wanted her to want to know him. Whether a relationship would come out of knowing Kate, he couldn't predict. But he was going to enjoy the process of finding out.

With a light step, he headed into the hospital, stopped by an empty consulting room, and pulled his compact cell phone from his sports coat. Why not call her at work? The invitation he had to offer in a way had to do with her job.

He consulted his pocket organizer for the station number and asked for her when a reporter in the newsroom answered the phone.

"I meant to ask you when I saw you, but you got away too

fast," he said. "Jacob, the little boy whose dog was hit, called me at the office today. His grandparents would like to have us over for Sunday dinner to thank us for helping with the dog."

"I didn't help," Kate said. "I just kept the camera rolling."

"It gave them publicity, and Jacob was thrilled to be on the news."

"If they want me, then I should go," Kate said. "What's their address? And what time?"

That wasn't quite the response he wanted. He'd hoped she would jump at the chance to be with him, but at least she was willing to go.

"Why don't I pick you up," he offered. "Around twelve-thirty?"

Kate agreed, gave her address to him, and then said she had to get back to work.

Well, that had gone fairly well, he thought as he walked into his grandmother's room and kissed the old woman on the cheek. She was still hooked to a heart monitor and an IV, but her color had returned, and her eyes were alert, even though her speech was somewhat garbled. Some words he could make out, but not many. He sensed her frustration in her eyes.

"Why don't I talk, Grandmother? I know it's hard for you like this, but the doctors say you'll regain your speech. It'll just take time."

He told her about work, about going on the rig with a driver the previous week when he was learning about the trucking industry.

"I'll spend the next few weeks at WKYS. I watched a remote newscast tonight from the mall. Did you watch the news?"

She gave a faint nod.

"I'm taking Kate Malone to dinner on Sunday."

Her eyes widened at that bit of news, and she made a noise that sounded like a protest—not the actual words, but the sound was an alarmed sound.

"She's smart and articulate," he said, "besides being beautiful. I thought you'd approve."

Grandmother shook her head.

"But why?" He knew he shouldn't upset her, shouldn't push an issue that obviously drew a negative reaction from her, but he couldn't understand what she would have against Kate Malone. And he wanted to know. It was preposterous to think that a glimpse of him as an unidentified Good Samaritan on TV could have this effect on her.

Grandmother said something that he couldn't make out, but her tone was unmistakable. She was displeased. Grandmother had been his confidant and his champion during his high school and college years, when his parents had tried to fit him into the social image that they thought appropriate. They'd even tried to pick his friends for him—from other wealthy families, of course. That Tyler and Joel had become close friends had annoyed them. To give his mother credit, she'd come to like Joel, but his father had never accepted him.

Grandmother had said that Tyler was like her late husband—a risk taker, a reckless sort, the type who could take a fledgling business and build it into a multi-faceted corporation. But Tyler hadn't wanted to go into the family business. His father's only participation in the corporation was to do the correct social thing, make hefty donations to charities, and attend board meetings as a principle stockholder. Tyler's mother had fit in with that image, and so had Vince.

Tyler had wanted to fly. He wanted to take charge of his life, live it on the edge, one day at a time, not walk the correct social walk. And Grandmother had helped him smooth the ruffled feathers of his parents when he went too far. The day he told them he had enlisted in the air force was etched in his memory. The old gal had defended him. Grandfather had served in World War II and had been a better man for it, she'd told them. Let Tyler live. Let him march to a different drummer.

Of course the drummer in the air force was the same one the other soldiers marched to, but as a pilot, Tyler was one of the glory boys, and he delighted in it. He flew through the ranks and would have made a career of the service, aiming toward the Pentagon, had Vince not died.

Since Vince had been merely the same titular leader as his father, Tyler was stunned when Grandmother asked him to come home and run the business. She said it was time a Sinclair took charge.

His commander was speechless when Tyler told him he wasn't re-enlisting. Tyler had served four tours, twelve years, and he was a major, on his way to becoming a very young lieutenant colonel. To throw that all away to be a civilian, the post commander had said, was foolishness. But Tyler had been adamant. He'd joined the service to be his own man. He'd done that. Now it was time he paid his dues to his family.

Grandmother had said take charge, and that's what he'd done. He was used to being in charge, and he liked it. Although the first few months had been rough, now that he had a new routine and was knowledgeable about the corporation, he felt confident that his decision to do as Grandmother had asked was a good one.

He was actually more in charge than he'd ever been in the service. He was his own boss. Sure, he would eventually answer to the board, but that was a rubber stamp of approval since the Sinclair family owned over half the stock. In the air force, there had always been a superior officer. Tyler felt the responsibility of his employees' jobs, but he was making the best decisions he could based on knowledge he'd recently acquired about the companies. He only had two more businesses to research. WKYS and a wholesale florist. He'd certainly turn his attention to the TV station next, learn more about Kate in the process, then he'd get into flowers. There couldn't be anything in the flower business that would alarm Grandmother.

She was still looking at him with that piercing stare, as if she could make him understand her objection to Kate, and then she said something unintelligible and turned her gaze to the door.

"Hello, Mother. Been to dinner?" Tyler asked.

Alma Sinclair nodded, walked toward the bed, and took the old woman's hand. "How is she?"

"Looking better," Tyler said. He wasn't about to say that he'd upset her by mentioning his date with Kate. "But probably tired out. Shall we let her sleep a bit?" He motioned his mother to the hall, and when they were out of Grandmother's earshot, she filled him in on the doctor's latest findings.

"She can go home as soon as we find a full-time nurse. He gave me the names of several agencies." She pulled a list from her purse and handed it to him. "He wants her to have a speech therapist, too, and a physical therapist."

"I'll see what I can do," Tyler said and glanced at his watch. "I'll call you later." He walked back into Grandmother's room and kissed the sleeping woman good night.

☙

"I want to look my very best," Chelsea said and paused in front of a dress shop window. "What do you think of this skirt? Maybe in pink. That color's good for me."

"Joel will be impressed if you wear your worst color," Kate said, "but I'm happy to give a second opinion, as long as I'm back by one. I need to unpack a few more boxes." She wanted the living room arranged and the pictures hung. It was time to do it, and she wanted to impress Tyler when he picked her up tomorrow.

When he'd first mentioned the thank-you dinner at Jacob's grandparents' home, she'd been afraid it would include Debra

Bowman. After all, she was the one who had interviewed Jacob at the veterinarian's office. Tyler hadn't asked to speak to her at the station, but he'd talked to Debra at the mall, so he could have invited her then. Kate hadn't thought of a diplomatic way to find out if the other reporter was coming, too. Well, she'd know tomorrow when he picked her up.

"What are you wearing for your dinner?" Chelsea asked as they walked down the mall to another dress shop.

"Whatever I wear to church, I guess. I won't have time to change before he picks me up."

"Go to early church."

That was something to consider. Kate had been visiting different churches before deciding which one she'd join. When she got back to her duplex, she'd check the church directory in the Saturday paper and find one that had an early service.

The shopping trip took longer than she expected, since they hadn't found anything perfect for Chelsea before taking a break for lunch. Then they both found new outfits—Chelsea's skirt and short-sleeved sweater in the newest fashion area, and Kate's fifty-percent-off forest green dress in the sale aisle. It was long-sleeved and slim-skirted, and it looked great with the reddish cast to her hair.

"Have a wonderful time tonight," Kate called to Chelsea when around three she finally dropped her off at the duplex. "I want to hear all about it."

Chelsea waved, and Kate turned back to her white-walled apartment. What could she do to make it hers? It desperately needed color. Her green couch and two low chairs that were grouped in a conversation area in front of the fireplace provided some relief from the white, but the place needed a splash of zap.

She walked around the room, looking at it from this angle and that and finally snapped her fingers. She would do it. She'd paint an accent wall. That couldn't take long, and if the landlord didn't like it, she'd repaint it white when she moved out.

The paint store had too many colors to choose from, but she quickly ruled out blues and yellows and settled on a rich burgundy. Armed with a sponge paint pad and a brush, she tackled the wall opposite the fireplace.

The color was exactly right, but it would take two coats to make it cover that white. While the first coat was drying, she sorted through pictures and unpacked books. She dragged a bookcase from her extra bedroom and artfully filled it with books and an occasional knickknack. She used the antique camera her grandfather had given her as a bookend on one shelf. On another she propped up a picture her eight-year-old nephew had painted. She laid books on their sides to use as bookends on other shelves and added a plant to another shelf. When she finished, she stepped back and admired her work.

"Not bad," she said aloud. Night had fallen long before the mandatory four-hour drying time was up and the wall was ready for a second coat. Kate carried her bedroom lamp in for added light, then painted the wall again. The second coat went faster, and by ten o'clock she had washed out the paint brush and pad and picked up old newspapers off the floor.

She turned on TV and watched Debra Bowman, who was filling in for the flu-bitten weekend anchor. Debra was a part-time reporter and noon anchor, and it was no secret that she wanted Kate's job. According to Chelsea, Debra had applied for it but had been ruled out as not experienced enough. Besides, rumor had it that John Yeager hadn't wanted to work with her, and he'd had a major voice in hiring a new anchor.

Now Debra was sending out her video tape, which was a reporter's resume, and Kate hoped she'd soon get a new anchor job and move out of Kentucky. After all, that was the goal of most TV personnel. Move up to a bigger market. Move to a bigger city. Move, move, move.

Kate glanced around her living room that now had a touch of flair. Since she'd fixed it up, would she find herself on the move again? And was that what she wanted? Indecision settled around her. She'd climbed her way up the ladder with honesty and candor, not fought her way up as she felt Debra was doing. Kate had lived by the principles she believed in. Number one was the Golden Rule. She treated others as she wanted to be treated. Even Debra. She might not like her, but she didn't pull any of the shenanigans that some reporters routinely stooped to, like not giving phone messages to the anchor or hogging stories that were called in from viewers.

Kate dismissed Debra from her mind as the weatherman came on the screen. Something had to be done about him. He usually did the noon weather, but he was helping out tonight because the weekend weatherman also had the flu. Kate wouldn't actually call it helping out. He consistently mispronounced names of towns and routinely pointed to the wrong area of the map.

After the news, Kate read more in McFee's book. If her assessment was correct that most writers included a bit of themselves in their main characters, especially in their first books, then Loren McFee had a ruthless streak. His attitude toward women was low-class, but then she'd only read part of one book, and she should read more before she developed a personality profile of the dead author.

He was certainly a powerful writer, and she picked the book up the next morning while waiting for time to leave for church. She'd decided late church was fine, since she'd wear her new dress to it and to dinner with Tyler.

Even McFee's riveting characters couldn't keep her attention as her thoughts turned to Tyler Sinclair. Her feelings for him rode a see-saw, first up then down, up then down. Of course, she'd only spoken to him a few times and for a few minutes each time. Today perhaps she'd get to know the real man.

She headed for a new church and found it with little trouble. Her own denomination was well represented in Bend, and she wondered why there were so many churches. Or maybe she didn't want to know. She'd long ago shook her head over the squabbling that went on in some churches. Perhaps it was human nature to be embroiled in power struggles, and churches were no more exempt than TV broadcasting.

She parked her car and walked up the broad walkway to the church. The outside of the old stone church looked newly sandblasted. The off-white stone was free of dirt and mildew. Inside was as immaculate as the outside, and it was nearly full, too. The sanctuary was not large, holding two hundred people at most. An organist played solemn music while the congregation sat quietly.

There were a few empty places at the back of the church and an empty pew near the front. If she hid at the back, she'd have little opportunity to meet many people, so Kate opted for the empty pew. She walked down the slanted aisle and gave a friendly smile to those who turned to look at her as she walked by. She felt as if all eyes were on her when she scooted to the end of the empty pew, so other latecomers could sit there, too. Did all these people recognize her from the news or were they merely looking over a perspective member?

She took a hymnal from the holder on the pew ahead of her and flipped through it, comforted to know the same songs were sung no matter which church she attended.

A couple minutes later she heard a gasp and looked up to see Tyler Sinclair and his mother sliding into the pew.

She hoped she didn't look as dumbfounded as Mrs. Sinclair. Tyler had an amused look in his eyes.

"Good morning," she said in a low voice. "I didn't know you attended this church."

He smiled. "Sinclairs have attended this church for over a

hundred years. And they've sat in this pew."

Kate pointed to the worn wooden pew. "This pew? This is reserved for Sinclairs?" He nodded. Now she understood the congregation's interest in her. How dare she defy tradition and sit in the Sinclair pew?

"Should I move?" She made a movement to rise, but he placed his hand on her arm.

"Stay put. There are only two Sinclairs here today, and there's plenty of room. My grandmother is absent."

"How is she?"

"Resting at home with round-the-clock nurses."

"Good."

The minister took his place at the front of the church, and the choir filed in from a side door as they sang the opening hymn.

Kate did her best to listen to the minister, but her mind wandered to the man beside her. She caught snippets of the sermon.

"Each one should test his own actions. Then he can take pride in himself, without comparing himself to somebody else."

She didn't know from what context the minister had taken the quote, but she applied it to herself and Debra Bowman. Did she compare herself to Debra? Yes, and she felt threatened by her, too, and she shouldn't. After all, Kate had landed the anchor job, not Debra.

"C. S. Lewis said, 'A proud man is always looking down on things and people; and, of course, as long as you're looking down, you can't see something that's above you.' How can we apply his notion to our own lives?" the minister asked.

Kate didn't think she was a proud person. She was proud of her accomplishments, but she didn't see herself as haughty. She would say she verged more toward humble than proud, although was it proud to think that way?

She couldn't think. That was her problem. Tyler Sinclair's proximity was disconcerting.

She stood with the rest of the congregation for the final prayer. As soon as the minister gave the benediction, friendly voices greeted one another, a different mood than the somber one before the service.

"Mrs. Sinclair, forgive me for sitting in your family pew," Kate said. "I didn't know it was reserved."

"Oh, it's not ecclesiastical law," Tyler said before his mother could respond. "Is it, Mother?"

Alma Sinclair smiled tightly. "No, of course not."

"I hope your mother-in-law is improving." Kate tried to make conversation, but she had an unwilling partner.

"Yes, thank you," Alma said and turned to speak to another member of the congregation.

"Shall I follow you home?" Tyler asked.

"That'll be fine," Kate said. "Or I could follow you to Jason's house."

"No, I'd rather we arrived together," Tyler said, and Kate was relieved that he felt that way.

He put his hand possessively at the small of her back and ushered her up the aisle, taking time to speak to a few people as they slowly made their way to the door. He introduced Kate to the Reverend Henry Crossland, who said he recognized her from the news.

"I always watch WKYS," he said.

"I'm glad we have a loyal viewer," Kate said, and then realized he watched the station because the Sinclairs owned it. "And I enjoyed your sermon," she added as they moved out of the way so others could speak with him.

Tyler walked her to her car, then followed her home. Once she had parked her car, he helped her into the passenger side of his car and climbed behind the wheel.

"Alone at last," he said and grinned across at her.

*six*

It was the first time she'd seen him smile like that—a Cheshire cat sort of grin—and she liked it. She grinned back.

"It's nice of you to give up time to see Jacob's family," she said.

"Have to check on the dog," he said with a shrug. "That mutt's a fighter."

"Do you have a dog?" Kate asked. She sensed his interest in the dog was more than casual.

He shot her a guarded glance, more like the countenance she was used to seeing. "I had one once."

"Me, too," Kate said, looking back in time. "When I was five, old Blackie disappeared. I thought she'd run off, and I couldn't understand why she'd do that, because we were pals. It was years later that my folks told me the vet had put her to sleep because she was so sick. They thought I was too young to understand. I wasn't. I could have dealt with the truth better than the thought that Blackie had deserted me."

"I made the decision to put Lucky to sleep," Tyler said. "It was the humane thing to do, but I cried."

Kate covered his hand that rested on the console with hers.

"The only other person who knows that is Joel," he said. "I don't know why I told you."

"Because I understand your pain," Kate said simply. She patted his hand and then drew hers away.

Tyler pulled into the Fullmers' drive, and Kate saw Jacob sitting on the front porch, obviously waiting for them. Woody sat beside him, his leg still in a splint. His tail thumped a steady rhythm on the wooden porch.

"Hi, Mr. Sinclair." He smiled a welcome at Kate, and Tyler introduced them. "I've seen you on TV," Jacob said shyly. "Come on in. Grandma's waiting."

He held the screen door open so that Kate could enter first. The living room was much like her grandmother's home in Illinois. Too much furniture crowded the small room, and knickknacks collected from years of special events and places cluttered end tables and a corner curio cabinet. A multicolored afghan was draped over the back of the couch, and Kate could imagine Jacob wrapped in it watching Saturday morning cartoons. The room had a cozy, lived-in feeling, and it was full of love.

Mrs. Fullmer, the same woman who had been with Tyler when Woody was injured, bustled into the room, followed by a man who looked exactly like a grandfather should—a little heavy, round face, kind eyes, and a big smile.

After introductions, Mrs. Fullmer ushered them to the dining area of the kitchen. Five places were set at the table. So Debra Bowman was not invited to this thank-you dinner. Kate's smile widened.

"Let me get you something to drink," Mrs. Fullmer said. She seemed ill at ease, and Kate realized she was seeing her as a TV celebrity and not as a normal person.

"I'll give you a hand," Kate said and crossed the room to the kitchen counter. "You know, these butterfly canisters are very similar to the ones I have. My mom made mine. Are you into ceramics?"

"I go to a class on Thursday mornings," Mrs. Fullmer said. "I've made decorations for every holiday. We sell some of our crafts for Santa's Helpers." She explained about the group she belonged to that bought toys for needy children. All year long they raised funds.

"Has the station ever done a segment on your group?" Kate asked. "We could do a Christmas in July feature, to show how you work year-round for the kids."

"Could you do that?"

"I don't see why not. I'll have to clear it with our producer, but he's very community oriented."

Mrs. Fullmer chatted on about the group while she and Kate put ice in glasses for tea. Kate glanced over at Tyler and saw that he and Mr. Fullmer were seated at the table and Jacob was showing them some baseball cards.

"I put this roast in before Sunday school," Mrs. Fullmer was saying as she fiddled with hot pad holders. "It should be done."

Mrs. Fullmer let Kate stir the gravy while she mashed the potatoes.

"Jacob lives with you?" Kate asked in a low voice.

For a brief moment Mrs. Fullmer suspended the potato masher before continuing with her work. "Yes." She hesitated just a moment, then said in a low voice, "My daughter's in prison. She got into drugs and wrote hot checks. We don't know where Jacob's father is. He deserted Tara before Jacob was born."

"I'm sorry," Kate said and touched Mrs. Fullmer's arm. "Perhaps this is the best thing for Tara. She can get treatment and come out with a second chance at life."

Mrs. Fullmer smiled, but her eyes glistened. "I don't know where we went wrong. We gave her a good Christian upbringing."

"In time she'll come back to her roots," Kate assured her. "You're not to blame, you know. Did you let your parents influence every decision you made at Tara's age?" She didn't know how old Tara was, but she knew that adult children made their own choices and had to live with them. She'd seen her aunt go through the same type of mental anguish when her daughter had strayed into alcoholism. Linda had joined AA and had made a new life for herself, but it hadn't kept her mother from beating herself up mentally and taking the blame for Linda's choices.

Kate knew that it was because she wasn't a mother and didn't have emotional ties to a child that she could have such a distanced view of the situation. Her aunt had told her many times that she didn't understand the heartache.

"No, I didn't blame my mother for my choices," Mrs. Fullmer said with an odd look on her face. "I never thought of it that way, and I don't know why I told you about Tara."

"I'm glad you did. It helps me know you better," Kate said. "I think this gravy is ready. Are we ready to take it up?"

Together they put the food on the table, then Mr. Fullmer asked the blessing. Dinner conversation bounced from topic to topic, and over dessert, Jacob asked Kate about her job.

"Would you like to come to the station sometime and see where we broadcast the news? I've got to warn you, it's pretty fake," Kate admitted. "Camera angles make things look bigger than they are, and our sets have a different feel when you're not looking at them on a TV screen."

"I'd like to see the little house where Sandy Moore does her show," Mrs. Fullmer said.

Kate laughed. "You're going to be shocked. It looks like a house, but it's just a few kitchen cabinets in one corner and a couch and chair in another corner. TV is an illusion. But you have to see it to believe it."

"I'm going to visit the set soon, too," Tyler said.

"You are?" Kate asked.

"I'd like to know the inner workings of all our companies," he said but didn't explain to the others that Sinclair owned WKYS. "When are you out of school?" he asked Tyler.

"Eleven-thirty. I go to morning kindergarten."

"Could you bring him out to the station on Wednesday?" Tyler asked Mrs. Fullmer. "We could watch the noon news and *The Sandy Moore Show*."

"That's a wonderful idea," Mrs. Fullmer said. "We'll go right out after I pick up Tyler. This is so exciting. I'm so glad you asked if Kate could be included in our dinner."

Kate looked questioningly at Tyler, but he avoided looking at her. So, it had been his idea to ask her to dinner. Most interesting. Was this his way of asking her out? No, the powerful head of the Sinclair Cooperation wouldn't need an excuse to ask someone out if he wanted to. He probably preferred company when he was forced to visit people he didn't know, and since she had gotten him so involved because of that video tape, he felt it was her duty.

They left soon after they finished their chocolate cake. Tyler made the excuse that he needed to check on his grandmother, who was ill.

"So, you suggested that I come along?" Kate asked, once they were headed back to her duplex.

"It seemed like a good idea. I figured it was work related, so you would go along with it."

"Oh." So she was right that he wanted a dinner companion for a dinner he wasn't crazy about attending.

"It worked," he said, and that grin of his was back. "You came, and I'm glad you did. You and Mrs. Fullmer got along well."

"Did you know that Jacob's mother is in prison?"

"So that's why he lives with his grandparents. What's she in for?"

Kate explained what she knew. "Mrs. Fullmer blames herself."

He nodded. "Most parents do. They're too close to the situation to see that adults make their own choices."

"How uncanny. That what I told her," Kate said. "Exactly what I told her."

He shrugged. "I've made my own choices in life, with God's help. I suspect you have, too. Not that we haven't had direction from our parents, but their direction isn't always the direction we want to go. We have to find our own places in the world."

Kate wanted to explore that further, but he pulled into her drive. Before she could get out, he was around the car and opening her door.

"Would you like to come in for coffee?" she asked.

"I'd love to, but I told Grandmother I'd be by around two. Could I have a rain check?" They had reached her door, and he stood beside her while she unlocked it.

"Sure," she said.

"Oh, and one more thing," he said and put his hand on her shoulder.

She looked up at him, questioning his gesture, when he lowered his head and kissed her.

It wasn't a long kiss; it was a touching of lips with a promise of more.

"I've wanted to do that since I first saw you," he said.

Kate stared at him dumbfounded and could honestly have said the same thing back to him, but she remained silent.

"Thanks for going with me today. I'll see you on Wednesday at the station."

She nodded, and he left.

Inside her duplex, she put her fingers to her lips. Had she imagined his kiss? Not likely. She would never have imagined something that tender and so full of promise.

She looked around at her newly decorated living room. He hadn't even stepped inside the door. If she had done this merely for him, her efforts had been wasted. But Kate didn't do things merely to impress others. Tyler may have been the impetus, but she had done this for herself. She needed her own sense of place in the world, a sense of home. And she now felt comfortable in this room.

She saw the answering machine blinking and smiled as she

listened to Chelsea's excited voice.

"Call me when you can. Lots to tell you."

She dialed her friend, who wasn't alone.

"Joel and I are headed to the park. It's such a nice day out."

"Enjoy. If you end up my way, stop in and we'll talk," Kate said.

She didn't expect Chelsea to take her up on her offer and was surprised an hour later when the doorbell rang and she found both Chelsea and Joel on the stoop.

"Want to come have ice cream with us?" Joel asked. "I'll get you a double scoop."

"Hey, this is nice," Chelsea said and walked into the duplex and around the room admiring Kate's new touches. "When you unpack a few things, you really unpack. I love the color of this wall."

"Thanks. I'll tackle my bedroom next. Might as well get settled in."

"Might as well," Chelsea said. "How was dinner?"

"Quite nice. The Fullmers are kind people."

"That's not what I meant. How did it go with Tyler?"

Kate raised her eyebrows at her friend. She didn't want to discuss Tyler in front of Joel.

"Yeah, how did it go?" Joel seemed as curious as Chelsea. "Did Tyler call you at the station? I gave him your home number. I didn't think you'd mind."

"He called me at the station. The dinner was actually work related since I did the story on that dog."

Joel laughed. "Did he tell you that?"

"Sort of."

"Well, don't believe him. He's intrigued by you, but he's worried about sexual harassment."

"What?"

"You know. He owns the station, so you work for him. Did you feel obligated to go with him or did you want to go?" He looked at her as if that were the most natural question in the world, so she answered it.

"I wanted to go."

"Good. Tyler needs you. He needs to loosen up. He's not been himself since he came back to Bend. Too uptight, and he works too hard. The old happy-go-lucky Tyler needs to come back. And you can help him."

"You're sure of that?" Kate asked.

"Positive. Come on, let's go get some ice cream."

She didn't want to be a fifth wheel, but Joel didn't make her seem that way. Since she thought she might find out more about Tyler from his best friend, she climbed into the back seat of his car.

So Tyler was uptight, she mused, and he used to be happy-go-lucky. That would explain those grins she'd never seen before. They belonged to a side of him that Joel knew and wanted back. She'd like to see more of that side, too. Did that kiss belong to the side of him that was carefree? Could it also be a part of his serious side?

If she interpreted Joel's concern correctly, then Tyler Sinclair needed more balance in his life, and she'd love to be the one to help him get it.

She found out little more about Tyler that afternoon, but the next morning when she was at the library, she couldn't resist the urge to look in *Who's Who*. She wasn't surprised to find his name listed there.

He had been in the air force and had made major at a remarkably young age. That fit in with her opinion of him. Now that she thought about it, he had a military bearing, and it was more than his straight posture. He had a commanding air about him that she'd associated with being in charge of a corporation, but there was obviously more to it than that. She'd like to talk to him about his military career. He'd returned to Bend to take over the family business. Had he wanted to do that, or had he felt family responsibility? Since he'd become more serious than Joel thought he should be, she felt it was the latter reason.

She put away the book and turned her thoughts to the assignment which had brought her to the library. Although sweeps month wasn't until May, and she had five weeks left before it aired, she wanted to get her story on unsolved murders ready. She had a list of three murders in the area, but the one that intrigued her the most was Loren McFee's.

She made photocopies of the newspaper stories for the days immediately following the two other murders. One was of a young woman who'd been abducted from a local bar. Another was a stabbing of a homeless person in an alley. Both of the murders were within the last five years. But the one that she felt certain would capture the viewers' attention went back to 1959 when Loren McFee had been killed.

Of course, it was the headline. She sat in the dark reading room, turning the dial of the microfilm reader, engrossed in the story. It appeared to be a break-in gone awry, since the bedroom had been ransacked. Police felt the burglar was surprised by Loren McFee, who was killed by his own gun. Mrs. McFee had returned home and found her husband sprawled on the floor.

Kate gasped as she read the next paragraph. Mrs. McFee had called her neighbor, Sylvia Sinclair, who'd arrived just before the police. Sinclair. That had to be Tyler's grandmother.

The only thing missing was an antique diamond brooch. Most everyone in Bend had seen it at one time or another, since Mrs. McFee wore it on many occasions. It had been her mother's, and she'd inherited it only a year earlier. A five-carat diamond formed the center of a flower, with smaller diamonds surrounding it as petals. Police suspected the thief would take the jewels out of the unique setting and fence them independently.

Kate read the next few days of newspapers, and the story was recapped time and again, but no new details were given. She printed a copy of the story and returned to *Who's Who*. Sylvia Sinclair was not listed. Nor did the phone book have her name, but then her number was probably unlisted. Tyler's wasn't in there, either.

When she went to work at one-thirty, she was glad to find Tim Woolard's bout with the flu was over. She zeroed in on the assignment manager. He used to be a newspaper man, and he probably had contacts at the police department. She could interview someone there about the murders.

"Your best bet would be Lieutenant Rockwood. He's a good guy and will tell you what he can, although some police leads might be confidential."

"Who would I talk to about a forty-year-old murder?"

"Why cover one that old?"

"Loren McFee, the author on that stamp I covered last week. It's an intriguing story when someone famous is involved. I think our viewers would have inquiring minds over this one."

He nodded his head in agreement. "Rockwood's dad would be the one for that. He retired a good fifteen years ago, but I'll bet he was in the middle of that investigation."

Kate wrote down the name and checked the phone book.

"Hey, Kate," Chelsea called across the newsroom, making her way to Kate's desk. "I meant to call you last night, but Joel stuck around until after the news. He's wonderful. Good sense of humor, intelligent, kind. I took him to meet the family last night."

"Is that rushing things a little?" Kate asked.

"It was Aunt Betsy's eightieth birthday. We had a cake and candles. He was still around, so I asked him to go."

"Your great-aunt has always lived in Bend. Right?"

"Right."

"Think she'd let me interview her about the McFee murder?" Kate explained about her upcoming series.

"She loves to talk about the old days, and anything scandalous is right up her alley."

Kate wrote down her name and number in her notebook. This series might pan out to be something very special.

"Kate." Mike Dodd sat down in the chair by her desk, and he was frowning. "Know anything about Sinclair coming out here?"

"You mean on Wednesday?"

"Yeah. He said he wants to learn how each of his companies operates. We're next on the list. Says he might be in and out of here for a few weeks. How'd you know he was coming Wednesday?"

"He asked the boy of the dog accident fame to come out and watch the noon news."

"That's when he's going to start learning the ropes out here. He says he's finishing up at Sinclair Trucking. He even went on a road trip. You think this is legit?"

"What do you mean?"

"You think he's been doing this for all his companies?"

"Tyler Sinclair wouldn't lie." It raised her hackles to think that Mike would doubt Tyler's motives. She felt protective of him, and she needed to think about that reaction.

"None of the other Sinclairs did anything like this. Not his dad and not his brother. I thought it might be getting us back for you doing that dog story."

"I think he's his own man, and I don't think he's out to ambush us. He just wants to know what he's in charge of. I think it's an admirable thing for a CEO to do."

Mike rose from the chair. "He'll be in first thing Wednesday. I'll get Debra to show him around. He can tag along with her and then watch her do the news. If he wants to see another broadcast, he can come in later the next day and watch you."

"Actually, you might want to let Sandy Moore be his guide." Now Kate felt possessive of him. What was wrong with her? "The boy's grandmother is coming to see Sandy's show."

"I'll make sure they're introduced, but Sandy doesn't come in until around eleven-thirty. Debra can take care of him," he muttered as he left her desk.

She was sure Debra would take care of him, and she didn't like it, not one bit. Kate checked the assignment board and discovered that Debra was out on assignment right now, and since almost everyone was back from the flu, she would be off work at five.

Tim called the daily meeting, and Kate pulled her chair into the circle to bat around stories and see what needed to be completed. It was another slow news day, and Tim was scrambling for ideas.

"The Humane Society will bring out another animal," he said. That was a standard when there wasn't much news. It gave needed publicity to the shelter, and usually the pet featured would be adopted. It wasn't Kate's favorite part of the news. John Yeager didn't like pets, so the honor of holding the animals went to her. Although she'd only been working at the station for a few weeks, already she'd been wet on several times and nipped once by a dog. The bright lights in the studio seemed to scare the animals.

At news time before the final segment, a small dog was brought in. This one was a cutie, but he was the worst of all. He threw up on her. He was sitting on the news desk, facing her, when he did it, so she hoped the viewers didn't see what happened.

"I'm going home to change," she said as soon as the camera light went off. "Poor thing must be sick. Could someone bring me some paper towels?"

The shelter worker took the animal. "We'll have the vet

look him over," he said and hurried out.

Chelsea flew in the studio with a handful of towels.

"Yuck!" she said and covered her nose with her hand.

"I'm leaving," Kate said as soon as she got the worst off. She had the fleeting thought that the animal shelter bit should be moved to the noon news.

Tuesday went much the same way—no real stories she could sink her teeth into, but at least there were no sick dogs. She called the shelter and learned that the dog was now fine and someone had adopted it.

She arranged a visit with the retired policeman for Thursday afternoon, and lined up a Friday morning visit with Chelsea's aunt. That would help her series, but even more pressing was Tyler's visit to the station on Wednesday. Should she go in early? Would that be too obvious? She could pretend that she went in to see Jacob and Mrs. Fullmer.

When Wednesday finally arrived, she tried on three outfits and discarded them. It really didn't matter what she wore; there weren't many colors that could clash with the navy-blue station blazer. She settled on a longish blue print skirt and a soft baby blue sweater. By ten-thirty she had drunk four cups of coffee and was tapping her fingers on the kitchen table. She'd finished the McFee books and decided to take them back to the library and get a couple more. From there, she might run into the station a little early.

Oh, who was she trying to fool? She was going in early. And she was going in to see Tyler Sinclair.

# *seven*

Kate walked into the station and plunked her purse in her desk drawer. There was no sign of Tyler or Debra.

"You're in early," Tim said from his desk. He didn't ask the question, but it was in his comment. Kate struggled to come up with a good answer.

"I was at the library and had some information on that unsolved murder series. Is there another series I should be working on for May? Anything else I need to research at the library?" Okay, that was a reach, but Tim seemed too preoccupied to analyze her reasoning.

"We'll do pet health and safety." He referred to his notepad. "Need to interview some vets. Maybe a different one each night on a different topic. You know the stuff—leaving them in a locked car on a hot day, feeding them table scraps."

"If I know it, won't pet owners already know it, too?"

"There are always first-time pet owners who need to hear it," he said, "but you might go for more obscure information. Can you give a cat too much tuna, that sort of thing."

Kate started a new page in her notebook for the series. "Any excitement around here?"

Tim gave her a searching look. "Tyler Sinclair's here. He's gone out on assignment with Debra. Should be back any minute."

Kate nonchalantly strolled over to the assignment board. Debra was at city hall for a routine news conference. The April election which would shake up the city council was right around the corner, and the council was giving out community service awards as a lame duck sort of thing.

Great. Now what could she do? She had nothing to edit, and she felt in the way. When the phone rang, at least she had a purpose.

"Newsroom. Kate Malone."

The call was a tip from a viewer. An injury accident had occurred downtown at Fourth and Main. A pedestrian had been hit. Kate took the name and number of the caller as a candidate for tip of the week.

"Anything on the scanner about a pedestrian accident?" she called to no one in particular. Most of the tips weren't true. She couldn't understand why people would call in tips to send reporters out on wild goose chases.

She walked over to the scanner and listened for any mention of an accident. Nothing came in. The phone book failed to reveal the name the tipster had given, and the city directory had no such person listed either. She dialed the number and got a machine that didn't have a voice like the caller. First National Bank was on that corner downtown. She looked up the number and called. No, there was no ambulance or police car downtown.

"False alarm," she said and wandered back to Tim's desk. "What about a series on financial planning? College funds, Christmas clubs, interest rates, that sort of thing?"

"Might work," he said and jotted it down.

Kate heard Debra's laugh from the hallway, and she picked up a local newspaper from the huge stack next to Tim's desk so she'd look busy.

"We could interview accountants, someone at a bank, someone from Edward Jones or A.G. Edwards. We might even get some of their clients to give us in-home interviews so we can have an expert assess their needs." She was spouting off the top of her head, all the while listening for Tyler's voice.

"Now I have to edit the tape," Debra was saying as she and

Tyler strolled into the news room. "You can go in an editing booth with me."

*Sure Debra would like him in one of those tiny dark cubicles with her,* Kate thought. Her conscience called her to task, telling Kate that her line of thinking wasn't in keeping with Golden Rule. But Debra didn't treat her that way, Kate's dark side argued.

Tyler smiled and strode across the room. "Good morning, Kate. Did you come in to help with Jacob and Mrs. Fullmer?"

"It'll be nice to see them again," Kate said noncommittally.

"Coming, Tyler?" Debra cooed.

"No, thanks. I'll get that lesson a little later."

"How's your grandmother?" Kate asked as Debra turned on her heel and in something of a huff headed to a booth.

"Improving little by little. Show me your desk," he said.

"Okay." Kate led the way to her little area. "Have you been on the grand tour?"

"No. I'll do the studio thing when Jacob gets here."

"Can I lobby for new equipment? New desks and a new ceiling?" She pointed up to the multi-stained ceiling tile. "The roof gets patched periodically. Icicles form on the tower anchor lines. With a little thaw and a high wind, they're blown straight down here. Tim says he's seen an icicle the size of a man's leg come through the studio roof."

"Dangerous," Tyler said. "Things are a bit rundown." He pulled a small notebook from his inside jacket pocket, wrote something, and then stuck it back in his sports coat. "Is there some place private where we can talk?"

"Tim's never in his office," she said, glancing over at Tim, who sat at a desk in the newsroom. "He likes being where things are happening."

"May I use your office for conferences?" Tyler asked Tim as they walked by.

"Oh, sure. Make yourself at home." Tim waved his hand

as if didn't matter to him.

Conferences weren't at all what Kate had hoped for. Tyler was treating her as he would any other reporter or anchor. Friendly, but businesslike. That wasn't what she wanted. She wanted a repeat of that tender kiss from yesterday. She let out a little gasp. What was she thinking?

"Right here," she said and figured he would take the seat behind the desk. Instead, he rolled Tim's desk chair beside the extra chair and sat down. She should have known his style of management wouldn't be to intimidate employees, but to talk to them as equals.

He pulled the pad out of his sports coat pocket again. "Now, Kate, everything you say in here is confidential. You're new here, but you've had time enough to learn who's doing his job and who isn't. Anything I should know?"

"You want me to rat on your employees?"

"No. I'm trying to learn what will make this a stronger station. I need an insider's opinion, and one I can trust. I'm not going to pull anyone else in here and ask the same question, although I am going to talk to others about what improvements we could make."

Kate pursed her lips in thought. Did she want to do this?

"Am I asking too much? Is this unfair?"

"No. I just need to think. . . The reporters are very capable, and they'll turn over fairly fast, if this is like a typical station. Okay, I'm going to tell you my opinion of one employee, but you have to judge him for yourself. The noon weatherman is not much of a weatherman. I'm not sure how long he's been here or what his qualifications are, but he regularly points to the wrong areas of the map and mispronounces town names. Surely he can't have been here long, or he'd know them."

There, she'd squealed on a fellow employee, and she didn't feel good about it. "He was nice enough to fill in last weekend when most of the weekend team was sick," she added so that there'd be at least one positive point in her report.

"I appreciate your candid assessment. Now what about Mike Dodd?"

"He's an excellent producer. Best I've worked for."

"Tim Woolard?"

"He loves this station. He works hard, and he's good at his job. You probably pay him for half the hours he works here."

"Sandy Moore?"

Kate smiled. "She's gone out of her way to make me feel welcome. She's tops at interviewing, and guests feel comfortable around her."

"Debra Bowman?"

Kate looked down at her hands. What could she say about Debra? How much was a personality conflict? Could she honestly say that Debra didn't do her job?

"Kate? What about Debra Bowman?"

"She's a competent reporter. She does fine on the noon news. Why are you asking me? You just spent the morning with her. What's your opinion?"

"She seems like an asset to the station."

That's not what Kate was thinking, but Debra certainly did her job. She might be a bit of a camera hog, but that wasn't that unusual.

"Anyone else?" she asked.

"Chelsea Cooper."

"She's a personal friend, so I can't be objective," Kate said. "But I think she does her job just fine."

"John Yeager?"

"He's an institution here. Probably been here longest of anyone, and that's most unusual for an anchor."

"Anchors move around?"

She laughed. "A lot. If they're doing a good job and have potential, two years at a station is a long time. John Yeager is quite an exception. He's found his place here."

"What about you? Is this your place?" He looked her straight in the eyes, and Kate felt he was looking into her heart.

"I don't know. Too soon to tell, I guess." She directed the conversation back to her co-anchor. "John and I get along fine. If one of us slips, the other one takes up the slack."

Tyler looked at her as if he knew she didn't want to talk about her future plans, but he kept firing names at her, and she gave her opinions. Once he paused, as if trying to think of other names, and glanced at his watch.

"We'd better go to the reception area. Jacob and his grand-mother may already be here," he said. They rose and made their way to the front of the station.

Through the entrance window, Tyler could see Mrs. Fullmer and Jacob just getting out of their car. "What timing," he told Kate. He'd been delighted that Kate was here when he returned from that assignment with Debra. Now there was a reporter who bothered him, but he couldn't put his finger on exactly why. She seemed the ruthless sort. This morning on location at city hall, she had vied for the best spot, getting in the way of other reporters' shots. But wasn't a good reporter supposed to be aggressive? He didn't think Kate would act like that.

He was well aware that Kate didn't want to answer his questions about personnel. Had he put her on the spot? Her assessments were right on target with his. The noon weather-man had bothered him for some time. Others seemed to be doing their jobs. He hadn't asked about Richard, the station manager, but he was someone Kate worked with on the peripherals. Richard should have been the one to weed out that inept weatherman.

Tyler held the outside door open for the Fullmers, and then Kate took charge of the tour of the station. She took them behind the scenes and introduced the engineer and the noon director, who were already in the booth.

Mrs. Fullmer was obviously thrilled when she met Sandy Moore, who did the noon interview segment. She pumped her hand.

"I always catch your show," Mrs. Fullmer said. "Since the beginning, I've watched it."

"That's saying a lot. I've been here twenty-two years," Sandy said. "I had no idea when I started that my show would last so long."

Tyler liked Sandy. He'd known her since he was a boy, more as an acquaintance than a close friend. These days they showed up at the same social functions.

"Excuse me, today's guest has arrived, and I need to get her a microphone," Sandy said.

Kate took them into the studio. Tyler had been in there when he was a kid, and it looked much the same, with each corner holding a different set. It was still as cold as he remembered it.

Jacob commented on the chill, too.

"So there's no little house for Sandy Moore's kitchen and living room," Mrs. Fullmer said. "Just pieces of one."

"TV is an illusion," Kate said. "Here's the green screen where the weatherman stands. He can only see the maps if he looks at the monitors on both sides of it." She let Jacob stand in front of the screen and pretend he was giving the weather. Both Jacob and Mrs. Fullmer sat in the anchor chairs. Jacob twirled around in his.

"Here, Tyler. Why don't you do the sports?" Kate asked and pointed to the chair.

"Now that's a job I'd like," he said as he sat down behind the long news desk. "Don't I get to go out in the community and take challenge matches?"

"You definitely watch our station," Kate said and laughed. "I think our sportscaster is playing darts today. Film on the six o'clock."

The sliding glass door opened, and Debra walked in.

"We'll get out of your way," Kate said, but took time to introduce the Fullmers. "Debra is the noon anchor."

"Oh, yes, I watch you every day," Mrs. Fullmer said and shook Debra's hand.

Kate ushered the group into the newsroom. "We'll watch the news from here. You can look at these monitors and see Debra live at the same time."

Jacob pushed his nose against the glass door. The cameramen took their positions, and someone turned on the huge lights. Mrs. Fullmer appeared as hypnotized by the scene as her grandson. Tyler stepped back to let them have a good view of the studio.

"It's really something," he told Kate. "Artificial in life, but it looks so real on the screen."

The noon weatherman was in the newsroom preparing to enter the studio with the first commercial break. Tyler felt Kate stiffen beside him. Maybe he shouldn't have asked her about incompetent personnel, but he'd wanted to know her thoughts.

He glanced through the glass at the noon anchor. He sensed animosity between Debra and Kate. He shook his head. There was no *sensing* about it. Debra had gotten in several digs against Kate when they were driving to the city hall assignment. He'd given Kate an opportunity to blast Debra, but she'd hesitated, and then she'd declined. He admired that.

The weatherman bobbled so badly that even Jacob commented on it. That was all it took. Tyler would tell the station manager to get rid of him. He didn't like making decisions like that, but for the good of the station—and that meant ratings and other employees' jobs—the noon weatherman was history.

Sandy Moore's segment was as professional as always. He'd wondered if that community spot would work better if she were teamed with a younger woman, but after seeing her in action, he knew that would be a mistake. She knew her viewers, and she catered to them.

"How about lunch?" he asked Kate in a low voice. "Shall we treat Jacob and his grandmother to a burger?"

"Why not? But I have to be back by one-thirty."

It was a quarter to one by the time they got to MacDonald's, Jacob's choice, but it didn't take long to eat. Tyler and Kate waved good-bye to the Fullmers on the station parking lot with minutes to spare before Kate was due at work.

Tyler pulled up a stool to listen to the assignments meeting, then he visited with various employees. The newsroom buzzed at a muted level, and he overheard a reporter, who'd just walked in ask why it was so quiet, then heard the low reply that the corporate boss was on the premises. At different times, he took employees back to Tim's office and talked with them, letting them tell him ways they could improve the station. Several had innovative ideas, and he jotted them down in his notebook.

He introduced himself to Chelsea Cooper when she came back in from an assignment. He knew who she was from seeing her at the mall. Joel was certainly smitten with her.

"Would you come into Tim's office?" he asked.

She sashayed inside and sat down. "I've heard a lot about you," she said. He raised his eyebrows in question, and she continued, "Joel thinks you hung the moon."

"Joel's right."

She laughed with him. He glanced up and caught Kate's gaze on the other side of the glass wall.

"What do you think of Kate Malone?" he asked. He hadn't meant to say that and wished he could take it back. "Never mind."

"That's okay. I think she could tell the sun to come up and it would."

"Well, you're a loyal friend to her."

"Yes, I am, and she's a wonderful friend to me."

He wanted to ask her about Joel, really wanted to warn her away if she was only toying with his affections. Two dates and Joel was head over heels. He'd called late last night, and Tyler hadn't heard him so excited about anyone since high school when one of the cheerleaders had led him down a rosy path and then dumped him. He didn't want that to happen to his friend again. But it wasn't his place to question Chelsea about him.

"What about Joel?" she asked. "Are you a loyal friend to him?"

"I hope so. He's a solid man, his character impeccable."

"He's a wonderful guy," Chelsea agreed. "He makes me laugh and want to sing. And I can't carry a tune in a bucket."

Tyler smiled. He could see why Joel liked her. She was straightforward and funny and cute as a button. He turned their little meeting to business and asked about the station and ways to improve it. When they finished, he asked her to send Kate in.

"Tyler?" Kate stood in the doorway.

"What are you doing after the six o'clock news?"

"I normally go to supper and work on anything that needs updating for the ten o'clock. This time I'm headed to a dinner meeting of the Hawthorne House, the center for abused women."

"You're doing a story on them?"

"Not exactly. When he hired me, Richard said it would be a good idea if I got involved in community activities, high profile stuff to benefit the station. I looked through a list of charities and groups and called Hawthorne House. They were searching for board members, so I applied. That's fast, I know, but I think they were desperate, and they thought I could give them publicity."

"Which you can," he said.

"Yes."

"And you attend board meetings on company time?"

"Yes. They're only once a month, and of course, I make sure I'm back here long before news time."

"That's probably a good policy. Otherwise it would be hard for you to join many organizations. Does John do likewise?"

"He's in a civic group that meets at noon, but he's on a couple of boards that meet at night."

"Well, if you're headed out, I guess I'll see if John wants to go to dinner."

"You mean I missed a dinner date?" Her eyes opened wide. "Sorry, I didn't mean a date-date."

"Actually, I did." He knew he shouldn't be asking her out on company property, but if she didn't want to go, surely she'd say so. "Are you free Saturday night for dinner?"

"I'd love that, but that's the night of the fund-raiser for the Boys and Girls Club. I said I'd attend."

"I bought a ticket for that. Chili and an auction later, right?" He hadn't planned on going, but if she was going to be there, he'd be there.

"That's right. I'm surprised you weren't hit up for a donation."

"I'm sure one of our companies is donating something. We're rarely left off a list. Would you like to go with me?"

"I'd love to."

"Around seven?"

"Perfect. Now, if you'll excuse me, I've got to do the five-thirty teaser."

He walked into the newsroom with her and watched her read the headlines. She was very good. She didn't appear to be reading from the computer screen, although she was. She talked to the viewer.

He watched tension mount before the six o'clock news.

Kate read news at her desk; John read news at his. Then they both slipped into their station blazers and walked into the studio.

This time he watched the news from the director's booth.

"Fascinating," he said, as he watched the director flip switches that cued up different video tapes. He listened while the director walked him through various steps, and he took a few notes, although he had no intention of ever doing this job.

"Is there a way of simplifying this?" he asked during a break. "Do we have the latest equipment?"

The director laughed. "We're in the dark ages in news equipment. No one at Sinclair has taken notice of us except during sweeps months to see if they can raise our prices for ads. During prime time, most of the commercials are national. But we get in a lot of local ads during the news. That thirty-second spot before the weatherman gives the forecast is our highest payer."

With the commercial over, the director focused on the screens in front of him and explained that dead air time or the wrong video with the script Kate was reading would be a disaster. Tyler admired the concentration and timing that went into the director's job. He slipped out of the booth and, at another break, walked into the studio and sat in a comfortable chair in Sandy Moore's corner.

Kate was a natural in front of the camera. It was in those eyes, just as Joel had said last week. She told the viewer what was happening because the viewer needed to know. She was the girl next door. Except she was a woman—a woman with laughing eyes, concerned eyes.

A realization washed over him, and he felt as if someone had punched him in the stomach. Kate Malone was going places. She could be an anchor on one of the network morning shows. She had the charisma, the charm, the intelligence.

And certainly the looks. That wasn't supposed to be so important these days, but it was, and no honest person in broadcast journalism would deny it.

At the next commercial break, he slipped out of the studio and went to the personnel office. It was empty, but he felt no guilt over rummaging in the file cabinet for Kate's folder. When he found it, he studied it carefully. She was twenty-six. She'd moved steadily up the ladder. Now that she had broadcast experience, she could climb those rungs at a faster pace. He was surprised she wasn't in a bigger market than this one. If she wanted, she could be in Chicago inside a year. A year after that, New York. So, why was she in Bend?

He slipped the file back into place and returned to the news room to watch the sports. At the end of that segment, the camera focused again on Kate Malone. She smiled at the camera and bid the viewing audience good night. "We'll see you at ten."

The lights were turned off, and while the credits ran, the news team sat in silhouette. Then the six-thirty sitcom rerun began.

John Yeager pushed the glass door open, and they all filed out of the studio. Kate quickly slipped on her coat and waved to the others. "I'll be back by nine," she said before she headed out the door.

"How about supper?" the sportscaster asked the others. "I'm starved.

Tyler ambled over by John. "Mind if I join you for dinner, John?" he asked. He had meant to go with the news team, but now he wanted to talk to the news anchor alone.

John glanced at the sportscaster and the weatherman, then shrugged. "Sure. Got a place in mind?"

Tyler mentioned a restaurant not far away where tall booths would insure a bit of privacy. He drove them in his Lincoln and passed the time talking about all he had learned that day.

"You've been around a long time," he said once they were seated and had ordered. "I remember watching you when I came home from college at breaks. I'll bet you've seen a lot of changes at the station through the years."

John rambled on about his family and why he stayed in the area and covered some of the embarrassing moments in front of the camera.

"You've seen a lot of women anchors come and go," Tyler stated.

"Oh, sure. If they've got ambition and they're any good at all, they move to bigger markets." He named one anchor who was now in Detroit. Another was in Cincinnati.

"How would you rank Kate Malone with the other anchors you've worked with?"

"She's bright, intelligent, wants to make sure she knows every aspect of the business. No one can beat her on the air. She sparkles. She started mid-February, and even though sweeps month was nearly over, the ratings increased. May will be her first full sweeps month, and I predict we'll go over the top."

"Think she'll stick around?" Tyler asked in as nonchalant a voice as he could manage.

"If she wants to. If she wants to leave, she could be in a top ten market by year's end."

# eight

Tyler was gone when Kate returned from her meeting. John said he'd hung around after supper, talked to the guys, then left. But he was back the next day when Kate reported to work at one-thirty.

"Is he still interviewing people?" Kate asked Tim.

"Since lunch he's been holed up with Richard."

Probably letting the station manager have it for keeping the noon weatherman on salary, Kate surmised.

She looked at the assignment board and checked a camera and tripod out of the equipment room.

"I'm off to interview Lt. Rockwood's father," she told Tim.

"He's an ornery old guy. A real character. If Rocky likes you, he'll talk. If he doesn't, you won't be able to pry a word out of him. Good luck."

The drive out to the country was pleasant on this sunny March day. Trees were budding and early jonquils bloomed on the south sides of houses. Kate found the Rockwood's mailbox and turned down the long lane. A fifties vintage ranch house sat beneath a grove of elm trees. Sitting in the sun on a metal lawn chair was an older man. His leathery face was wrinkled, and Kate couldn't tell if there were more frown lines between his eyes or smile lines around the corners.

She introduced herself and confirmed that this was David Rockwood.

"Been retired for over fifteen years," he said. "Sat behind a desk the last five before they put me out to pasture. What is it you want to know?"

Kate explained about the unsolved murder series. She told

him about the two more recent ones, then mentioned the Loren McFee murder.

The old man straightened in the chair. His eyes grew brighter, and his entire demeanor changed to one of sharp interest.

"What do you know about it?" he asked.

"Very little. I'm here to find out what *you* know about it. Do you mind if I record our conversation and use a bit on the news if it fits, Mr. Rockwood?"

"Go ahead," he said. "And call me Rocky."

Kate attached the camera to the tripod and focused it on him, and then she stepped in front of it and gave the date and the series name.

"Don't pay attention to this. It'll just run while we talk. Mind if I pull up that other chair?" she asked. He nodded at it, and she moved it closer to his.

"Were you involved in the investigation of McFee's murder?"

"Involved? My partner and I were the first to respond."

"What did you find when you arrived at the scene?"

"Mr. McFee had been shot by his own gun. Oh, he didn't shoot himself, that was obvious from the wound, and from the looks of things, he struggled with the killer. If we'd had the technology they have today, we could have nailed the killer. Could have gotten skin samples from under his fingernails and matched DNA."

"Did you see skin under his fingernails?"

"Didn't look. But he was scratched on the face, so I figure he gave as good as he got." He drew a series of lines across his face with his index finger. "Like this. On the right side of his face."

"Does that mean the killer was left-handed?"

He leaned his head to the side. "You taken some of those criminology courses?"

"No," Kate said and laughed. "Just read a few mysteries and watched a lot of police dramas. At the station, the TV's always on." She certainly didn't sit and watch TV at work and didn't know if she'd ever watched a police show all the way through, but she was a sucker for the courtroom scene when the lawyer discovered who had really committed the crime.

"Well, you figured right. The killer was left-handed."

"Any idea who the killer was?"

He looked hard at her and then at the camera. "None that I'm willing to say on film."

"What happened when you arrived?"

"Mrs. McFee found the body. She was nearly hysterical, and Mrs. Sinclair was trying to calm her down."

"Mrs. Sylvia Sinclair of Sinclair Corporation?" Kate held her breath waiting to hear his answer. She knew Sylvia had to be Tyler's grandmother.

"There's only one Sinclair family in town. Mrs. Sinclair still lives up on the hill. McFee's house is at the bottom. Mrs. McFee called her neighbor right after she called us, and she beat us to the scene."

"Any idea where Mrs. McFee lives now?"

"She left here shortly after the murder. Went to Illinois to live with her sister. I believe she remarried. Mrs. Sinclair could tell you. They were good friends, and I'll bet they haven't lost touch."

Kate wondered if Tyler knew Mrs. McFee. She made a note to ask him.

"What about the robbery?"

"Ha," he scoffed. "There was no robbery."

"A diamond brooch—"

"Oh, I know all about it disappearing, and that bedroom looked like it had been ransacked, but why dump out a bunch of drawers if you were looking for jewelry that was in a jewelry box?"

"Perhaps the robber was looking for something more. Other valuables."

"Then she should have looked in other rooms, too. The den, the living room, his office. Nothing else was disturbed."

"She?"

He smiled. "You're pretty quick. You want to turn off that camera?"

Kate sensed that he was going to say something important, so she jumped up and switched off the camera and put the lens cap on, just so Mr. Rockford would trust her not to record it.

"Somebody set out to kill McFee. I'm thinking it was a woman because of the scratch marks on his face. A man wouldn't operate like that. He'd have punched him, but not scratched him."

"Do you have an idea who it was?"

The old man rubbed his jaw. "I'm not ready to say, but now that you've brought this to light again, I might have to do a little investigating on my own. You know, McFee wasn't the nice man he let on to be. I have that on authority. There could have been a string of women who wanted him dead. And two of them were in the house with his body when I got there."

Kate's mouth fell open. "What are you saying?"

"I'm not saying anything yet. But I'm going to do a bit of checking around."

He had purpose in his eyes, and Kate felt it was best not to push him. She fished in her purse for her business card and handed it to him.

"When you find the murderer, will you call me?"

He laughed, a deep bass laugh, and Kate decided he had more wrinkles from smiles than frowns.

He helped her pack up her equipment, and she drove back to the station. Tyler was there, but she didn't have an opportunity to talk to him. He was still with Richard, and the grapevine said they were going over some numbers. What numbers they'd be looking at, Kate had no idea. She'd thought the profit and loss statement for the station would be at Sinclair headquarters, but perhaps each of his companies operated alone and merely fell under the umbrella of the corporation.

She read over reporters' scripts, edited one, and put changes into the computer. It was after the five-thirty teaser when she saw Tyler, and she was too busy rehearsing to talk to him.

During the news he roamed about as he had the night before. This time he started out in the studio, then went to the booth, and back to the newsroom. She was aware of his movements even as she read the news.

"Going to dinner?" he asked her after the camera's red light had disappeared and the bright lights had been turned off.

"Sure," she said. "I told the guys I'd go with them. Want to join us?" She leaned closer to him and whispered. "They rarely include me, so I couldn't say no."

"All right," he said, "but I'll drive."

"Like to be in control, do you?" Kate teased.

He nodded. "I guess I do."

The entire news team piled into Tyler's Lincoln, and he drove them to a nearby restaurant that specialized in chicken. Conversation was general and relaxed. Except for the sportscaster, the other men were older than Tyler and didn't seem to stand in awe of him.

"How do you like the station?" John Yeager asked.

"Seeing behind the scenes is quite an education. I've been meaning to ask, what do you think of the station blazer?"

"Keeps us from having to think of what to wear," the sportscaster said. He wore jeans with his blazer, since nothing above his waist showed behind the news desk.

"I've been looking at other stations, and those anchors don't dress alike. No uniform. I've also talked to some of our viewers, and they'd like to see Kate in something besides this." He reached over and tugged on her lapel. "One woman told me she watches Kathie Lee Gifford's show just to see what she's wearing each day."

"I'm no Kathie Lee," Kate said.

"No. Your Kate Malone, and you already have quite a following. Different clothes each night would give more variety. Richard can look into trading advertising time with some department stores and giving you each a clothing allowance. What do you think?"

"I'm not a frilly person, if you're thinking more feminine attire," Kate said slowly.

"Just whatever suits your personality. You get to choose. The lead-in to the news has you in several different settings and dressed appropriately. That green suit, the black dress, even the jeans. And your hair's fixed different ways. It lets viewers get to know the real you. I noticed the network morning news shows don't have station blazers."

"You've convinced me," the sportscaster said. "I've been thinking we could move me away from the desk and into a corner of my own. We could make the set look like a locker room or a coach's office and I could wear casual attire."

"Great idea." When the waitress brought the check, Tyler reached for it and treated everyone. "Since we've been talking business," he explained.

"Awfully nice of you," Kate said as they walked side by side out to the car.

"I wanted to take you to dinner, and I got stuck with this group. I'll remember this, Kate," he said with an easy laugh.

Tyler left shortly after returning everyone to the station.

"What's going on between you two?" John Yeager asked when Kate handed him his copy of several stories that had been left on her desk.

"Nothing," Kate answered.

"Is that why he made a point of sitting next to you?"

"It's a bad spot, but someone had to sit there," Kate said. "I also sat next to you."

"Yeah, but I didn't look at you the whole time we were eating."

"Maybe he's fascinated by her dinnertime manners." The weatherman had come into their area and obviously had eavesdropped. "Did you notice he didn't comment on what the rest of us wear in the intro? Or how my hair is fixed?"

"Do I smell romance in the air?" the sportscaster asked.

"You guys are making this up," Kate said. "If he wanted to take me out, he wouldn't have included you. He wanted to talk about wardrobe allowances. My intro is obviously more varied than yours. You're in a suit or slacks, John. Only you have on sweats and jogging clothes," she told the sportscaster.

She didn't know why she was refuting their claims. She wanted romance in the air; she wanted a repeat of that kiss she and Tyler had shared Sunday. But she didn't want to be on the receiving end of these questions.

"I wonder how much money he's talking about?" the weatherman asked. "I could use some new suits. And since the camera shows all of me, I'd have to dress right."

"We could use a new backdrop for the news," John Yeager said. "Why don't you ask him for one, Kate? I'll bet he would go for it."

"Yeah, and ask him for a new weather center while you're at it," the weatherman said. "I think our viewers are figuring out that half the stuff in my set is old computer equipment that doesn't work."

"Could you get me a raise?" the sportscaster asked. "I bet he'll do anything you ask."

"Enough, guys. Don't you have work to do?" Kate asked and turned her chair around to face her desk. The men took the hint, and soon the newsroom had resumed its normal frantic pace without all eyes focused on her.

Chelsea eased over to Kate's desk. "Couldn't help but over-hear. What's the scoop?"

Kate filled her in on the supper break.

"I met Joel for a hamburger," Chelsea said. "He's a great guy. The more I know about him, the better I like him."

Kate could say the same about Tyler, but she didn't know him all that well. Sure she felt an irresistible pull toward him, and she thought he felt it, too. But other than his church affili-ation, the way he treated his grandmother and mother and best friend, the kindness he showed the Fullmer family, the fairness he showed the station employees, and what she had read about him at the library, what did she know about him?

Actually, that was quite a bit. She also knew he was a good kisser. That wasn't as high on her list of characteristics for a spouse as other things were—a Christian man, good moral character, good provider—but it was a great side benefit. Oh, here she was thinking of him as she had the first day she'd seen him. Was she making up the attraction because she wanted it so badly? That was what had been missing from her life in Iowa and Minnesota. She'd never analyzed it, but she had been lonely at times. Tyler filled a hole that she hadn't known was there.

"I said, when are you going to see him alone?" Chelsea must have asked her before, but Kate had been lost in her thoughts.

"Saturday night," she said and explained about the fund-raiser.

"That's hardly alone," Chelsea said.

"It'll have to do for now," Kate said, but she made a mental note not to promise away all her free time.

The next morning, Kate took bakery muffins to Chelsea's aunt Betsy's house for her interview. She didn't take a camera this time, since she figured Aunt Betsy's information would be more along the gossipy kind and not something she could put on the news.

Her prediction was right. Aunt Betsy knew practically everyone in town, and that was a feat when the population was right around eighty thousand. She was an octogenarian all right, and she had gray hair, but that was the only one of Kate's preconceived ideas of what an eighty-year-old should be like that she met.

Her eyes were bright and lively, and she didn't miss a thing. She'd taught school for nearly fifty years, and she'd never married. If she didn't know a person, she claimed, at least she knew some of that person's relatives. Probably had them in school.

"Loren McFee was a case," she said. "I always suspected that his public side and his private side were miles apart, but I didn't know him except to see him at book signings and public events. His wife was the quiet kind. She didn't belong to any organizations that I know of, and I was in a good many. She stayed to herself."

"Were she and Mrs. Sinclair friends?" Kate asked. On this interview, she didn't even have her notebook out. She was fishing for feelings, something that would lead her to someone with concrete facts.

"Sylvia Sinclair is a good old gal," Aunt Betsy said. "She has more common sense in her little finger than the rest of those Sinclairs did in their whole bodies. Except the younger boy."

She had to be referring to Tyler. Kate would never in a million years refer to that tall man with the military bearing, intelligent eyes, and quick mind as a boy.

"Sylvia's had a minor stroke," Aunt Betsy said. "They're keeping it quiet, but I have my sources that say that's so."

Kate nodded, but didn't confirm or deny her words.

"That's too bad, too, because she's sharp as a tack. She

asked the younger boy to come back and run that corporation. She wants to make sure it's as strong when she dies as it was when her husband was in charge."

"Were she and Mrs. McFee friends?"

"They were neighbors. I think Sylvia went out of her way to befriend Jane McFee. That gal would have been too intimidated to make an overture to Sylvia. Loren liked his wife running with the Sinclairs. Meant he was included in all the big splashy parties in town, and that was mighty important to him. Being seen with the Sinclairs meant his picture was in the paper and he got more and more publicity."

"I thought the Sinclairs didn't like publicity."

"You don't see much about them now, but in the old days, it didn't seem to bother them. They were always doing this and that. Oh, I don't want to make it seem like they weren't doing for the community, because they were. They made Bend what it is today. Every charity was after Sylvia to be on the board because she'd donate money to their cause. Sylvia is a good Christian woman who believes in doing for others."

"Did Loren McFee also serve the community?"

"Loren McFee only served himself," Aunt Betsy said with a frown.

"You didn't like him," Kate stated, but it was actually a question.

"Not a bit. He acted too high and mighty."

"Who do you think killed him?"

"Don't I wish I knew. Why, I'd write a book myself if I could figure that one out. What got you on to it?" she asked with a sly smile.

"Not a lot, but a forty-year-old unsolved crime intrigues me. Do you know what happened to Jane McFee?"

"She moved away right after he was killed. Moved in with relatives in Illinois, but I'm not sure what town. I heard she remarried."

"Know her married name?"

"No, but Sylvia would know. When she gets better, maybe you could ask her."

*Or her grandson,* Kate thought.

She didn't get the opportunity that day, because Tyler didn't come into the station. Instead, he called the producer and station manager to a meeting at Sinclair Corporation headquarters.

"We're in for some big changes," Mike Dodd said when he returned. "He has ideas and wants to change our image."

"Clothing allowance?" John asked.

Mike nodded. "Among other things. We're going to get a new look and make the other stations sit up and take notice."

"Does that mean we can go shopping this weekend?" Kate asked.

"Not so fast. He wants hype to go with the new sets. New clothes will start when the new set is unveiled. He's got designers working on it but wants your input on it. Said each of you should put your ideas on paper and submit them to him on Monday. Down to how high you want the news desk and what you'd like to see as a backdrop."

Kate worked on her list on Saturday. She wanted to be realistic and not imitate other stations' sets, but at the same time she wanted the new set to be modern and reflect today's approach to the news. An upscale approach, that's what she wanted.

She thought about it as she dressed for the fund-raiser at the Boys and Girls Club. The chili feed wasn't a dress-up occasion, but she wanted to appear sophisticated and casual at the same time. She settled on navy slacks, a silky white blouse, and a tapestry-type vest of deep maroon with navy and forest green threads woven in intricate flower patterns.

Tyler's smile gave his approval when she opened the door to him precisely at seven. He had also struck the balance between casual and classic with a tweed sports coat and khakis.

"You look terrific," he said with a smile in his eyes. "Ready for chili?"

The large metal building that housed the Boys and Girls Club was filled with people eating at eight-foot long cafeteria tables and other guests looking for empty spots where they could eat. At one end on a raised stage, a gospel group with two guitars, a fiddle, and a keyboard played lively tunes. Displayed in front of them were items for the auction, which ranged from large bags of dog food from the local plant, to red Coke coolers, to a painting by a local artist.

Several people spoke to Tyler as they wove their way through the crowd to the end of the serving line. Kate smiled and said hello to others who spoke to her. They called her by her first name, but she had no idea who they were. That was the thing about being a local news anchor. She came into their living rooms every evening at six, and if she was doing her job right, they would feel that they knew her. One of her goals was to learn their first names, too.

When she stood beside Tyler Sinclair, she wanted to be part of this friendly community. He made her want to belong, want to stay in this location for the rest of her life. Made her want to forget the ladder of success in broadcast journalism and stay on her safe rung forever.

Within a few minutes they were served and found seats at a crowded table. The chili was hot and spicy.

"This probably isn't good manners," Kate said, "but I like crackers crunched up in chili. Do you mind?"

"I've never tried that, but I will," Tyler said, and dropped a saltine in his chili and cut it into pieces with his spoon.

How like him, Kate thought. She followed suit, instead of breaking the crackers in her hands and dropping them in the bowl, which was her regular way.

The crowd thinned before the auction, but Tyler sat near the front with Kate and bid on several items that Kate knew he had no use for.

"I thought you said you didn't have a dog," she said after he successfully bid on a giant bag of dog food.

"I don't, but I thought we could take it to Woody," he said.

Kate bid on a dinner sail for four, but dropped out when the bidding went over $150.

Tyler held up his bidding number and bought it for $320.

"I've never been sailing," he said. "But I'll bet it's an adventure."

"You'll love it," Kate said. "There's a lake near my hometown where some friends have a sailboat, and I've gone with them several times. It's the most relaxing thing ever—if you're not the captain."

"Then we'll have a relaxing time." After the auction, they met with the couple who donated the daytime cruise and arranged for the sail the following Saturday.

"If the weather cooperates," the owner said. "We need good wind and clear skies." He gave his card to Tyler, who listened to directions to the lake.

"Why don't we ask Joel and Chelsea?"

"Wonderful idea," Kate said. "I think they'll jump at the chance to go."

With the auction over, Tyler hoisted the large bag of dog food on his shoulder and carried it to his car.

"It's only nine-thirty," he said. "Do you think it's too late to take this over to the Fullmers?"

"We could drive by and see if there's a light on," Kate suggested.

Every light in the house was on, so they stopped, and Tyler unloaded the bag on the front porch. Mr. Fullmer answered the door and waved him inside, but he shook his head and gestured to Kate, who sat in the car.

"We were invited in," Tyler said as he slid into the driver's seat, "but I declined."

"It is late to go visiting," Kate said.

"But not too late to be invited in for coffee at your place," he said.

"Oh, no, not too late for that," Kate agreed.

When they arrived at her duplex, Tyler took her key and opened the door, then stood back as she walked in ahead and turned on a lamp.

"I'll put the coffee on," she said.

"Actually, we can skip the coffee," he said. "All I really wanted was to be alone with you." He took her in his arms and kissed her, and she felt as if she had come home. This wasn't a tender touching of the lips. This kiss was a full-fledged man to woman kiss, and Kate felt it all the way to her toes.

# nine

Sunday morning Kate argued with herself about church, but in the end her good sense won out and she set out to visit another church. Part of her wanted to go back to Tyler's church, but she'd told herself she would visit all those in her denomination before choosing the one which felt most like home.

As soon as church was out, she headed straight for Sulphur Springs, Indiana. The drive was about an hour, and her family was holding Sunday dinner for her.

Her oldest brother, Harold, who lived in Oregon, was home for a few days, and he rushed out to the car to meet her.

"How have you been?" he asked after he'd hugged her and swung her off her feet.

"Wonderful," she said. "Coming to see me?"

It was their standard joke. Harold made quick visits home to see their folks every few months, but he had never visited Kate. His work as an oncologist demanded his attention, and the times he dropped into Indiana were usually when he was on his way to or back from a conference.

"Yes, I am. Now that you're within reach, I'm taking you out to dinner tomorrow night. The best place in town. Can you go?"

Kate laughed. "I wouldn't miss it. I'll find the perfect restaurant." In her mind, she arranged her Monday schedule to allow for an extra long dinner hour.

She spent the entire afternoon with her family—admired her youngest sister Becky's dress for the senior banquet, played chess with her grandmother, walked around the yard with her mother exclaiming over newly opened yellow and red tulips and heavily blossomed redbud trees, argued with her dad over local politics, and drew a map so Harold could find the station Monday night.

All too soon she was driving back to Bend. There was nothing like a Sunday afternoon with family. She'd never thought so when she was young and had lived in Sulphur, but now that she'd been away, those lazy long afternoons beckoned her home. It was one reason she had taken the anchor job in Bend. Three of her grandparents had died while she lived in Minnesota. She wished she had held them closer, and she wasn't going to let Grandma slip away without letting her know how important she was.

When she got home, she unpacked the spinning spools quilt that Grandma had made for her and draped it over the couch. She had meant to get that out earlier. It looked splendid in the living room. The dark burgundy in the center triangles of each block matched the new shade of her accent wall. Perhaps that was subconsciously why she'd picked that color.

She'd hoped there would be a message from Tyler on the answering machine, but there were no messages at all.

He was at the station when she pulled in around ten on Monday morning.

"You're here early," Tim said as a greeting.

Kate explained about her brother coming to town and the hope that she'd get a long dinner break if she put in more hours before the news.

"Actually you came at the right time. Ginger Brett had her babies. The call just came in. She told everyone she was having triplets, but there are five, and they're identical."

Kate wasn't sure who Ginger Brett was. She'd not heard any talk about triplets, and certainly not quintuplets.

"Story at Mount Carmel?" she asked.

"Yep. Take Zip and interview the happy family."

"Frantic family might be more like it." There were five kids in Kate's family, but they were strung out over sixteen years, and still her family's household had been rambunctious. How would her mom and dad have managed if their children had all been the same age?

Kate handed Tim her written suggestions for a new set. "Would you see that Tyler gets these?"

"Sure. Now take off. We want this on the noon news."

Within minutes Kate and Zip were at Mount Carmel. She helped the cameraman carry in equipment and followed arrows to the maternity ward. Zip filled her in on Ginger and Brad Brett. Ginger had worked as a receptionist for the station until four months ago when the doctor had ordered her to rest. Brad taught chemistry at Bend's Northside High School.

"I wondered how long it would take before the TV station got here," a nurse said in the hallway. "Isn't it wonderful? Every one of them is healthy."

A group had gathered around the nursery window and watched as the babies were placed in incubators. Zip set up the tripod and took footage as Kate got random comments from the onlookers, most of them members of the Brett family.

"How long was your daughter on fertility drugs?" Kate asked Ginger's mother.

"She wasn't. These are miracle babies. No drugs. All girls. All identical. She wanted to have a natural delivery, but that wasn't possible. The doctor waited until her water broke, then did the C-section. She was awake the whole time. What will Ginger do with five girls?"

"Love each one individually," Kate said. This was a big story. Sure, there had been the septuplets born last year, but those were a result of fertility drugs. These were nature's own, all identical.

Kate spent nearly an hour talking to the doctors, nurses, new grandparents, and finally interviewing Ginger and Brad.

Back at the station, she ran for an editing booth. She had so much good material, and she knew she couldn't use a twentieth of it. She argued for four minutes of air time, an unheard of length for a news story, but Tim agreed since it was such uplifting news.

She handed the tape to the news director with only minutes to spare before the noon news, and she gave Debra a copy of the computer prompter sheet.

With satisfaction, Kate settled into her desk chair and watched the feature on the monitor.

"Wow!" Tim said at commercial. "I should have given you five minutes. I expected everyone to say the same thing, how wonderful it was, yadda, yadda, yadda. You're a good interviewer, Kate. This is big news."

That was high praise coming from Tim, and Kate glowed. "Thanks. What fun to do a story like this. Got anything else you need me to work on?"

"We're full staff again, so you're free to work on your series. Guess you earned that long dinner hour. How long are we talking?"

"Two hours, tops." That would give her time to show Harold her duplex and have a nice dinner. "Know any place fancy I should take him?"

"The French Hen is the most uptown. You out to impress him?"

Kate nodded.

"Better call for a reservation. Oh, I gave your set suggestions to Sinclair."

"What did he say?"

"Nothing. Just took them. I suspect they're the first he's gotten. Well, plus mine." Tim told her about his ideas for different sets for six and ten.

The news came back on, and Kate raised her eyebrows when she saw a new weatherman on the set.

"Who's that?" she whispered to Tim, even though their conversation couldn't be heard in the studio.

"New guy. Just trying him out. Have five scheduled for the next two weeks. Each one gets two days."

"Did George get the ax?"

Tim nodded. "About time. He was pulling the noon news down."

Kate agreed but felt a stab of guilt that perhaps she had caused Tyler to fire George. Surely Tyler had formed his own opinion about George's inability to give the weather. She'd like to talk to Tyler about it, but his car had been gone when she'd returned to the station. He'd probably be back in the afternoon to go over set design with the anchors.

"I'm going to get lunch," she announced. "Anyone want anything?" she asked no one in particular and took several orders. She drove to a nearby hamburger place. Within minutes she was back distributing fries and burgers and change.

While she ate, she got on the Internet and looked for more information about Loren McFee. She'd forgotten Saturday night to ask Tyler about Mrs. McFee's married name. Next time she'd ask for sure. She hated to call Mrs. Sinclair to ask. It might upset her, and she wouldn't risk that again.

A lightbulb went on over Kate's head. If it were possible for a news story to elevate Mrs. Sinclair's blood pressure to the point of a minor stroke, it wasn't an innocent picture of her grandson doing a good deed that had caused it. Her stroke had occurred during the ten o'clock news. The dog-at-the-vet story had aired then, followed by the dull stamp story. Dull to most viewers. Not dull to one person who would never want to hear the name McFee again. Hadn't Rocky told her that Mrs. McFee and Mrs. Sinclair were among a handful of women who would not be saddened by Loren McFee's death?

She had to talk to Mrs. McFee. Was there any other way of getting that name? She got up from her desk and paced to the vending machine and back, thinking.

Debra was sitting at her desk when Kate returned to the newsroom.

"That was some story on the quints," Debra said.

"You ought to see those babies. They're so tiny, but they're all breathing on their own. Only two weigh slightly less than three pounds."

Kate dug some change out of her purse and returned to the vending machines for a soft drink. A minute later she walked back, still thinking of how to locate Mrs. McFee. Above the static of the ever-present scanner, she heard Debra say into the phone, "Kate Malone isn't here right now. Perhaps I could help you."

Kate crossed over within Debra's sight and said, "Is that for me?"

Debra looked a bit embarrassed, but quickly recovered. "Oh, she just walked in. One moment." She pushed the hold button.

"I thought you'd left," she said.

*Not likely,* Kate thought. She'd left her computer on, and her purse was in plain sight beside her chair.

"Kate Malone," she said into the phone. She motioned for a reporter to turn the scanner down and listened as the producer of the network morning show in New York asked about the Brett quintuplets.

"Of course," Kate said. "I'll be at the hospital at five-thirty with the satellite feed. Thanks for calling."

All eyes in the newsroom were on Kate when she hung up the phone. "That was New York," she said. "The network's doing a story on the quints on the morning show."

"And you're doing the live shot," Debra said with a touch of belligerence in her tone.

"Yes." Kate walked to Tim's office where he was holed up, an unusual place for him. "Did you call the network?"

His eyes lit up. "I fed the video to New York while you got lunch. So they want the story?"

"A live shot tomorrow morning. Think those babies will want their pictures taken with their parents?"

He laughed. "Can't predict babies, but I imagine Ginger can be convinced if she's feeling all right. Better head out there and find out."

Tyler was pulling into the lot when Kate walked out the side door. She waited beside his car for him to get out. Her initial reaction to seeing him again was to reach for him, to hug him, but she restrained herself and tried for a professional, not personal, air.

"Hi, Tyler. Your station's going to be on network television tomorrow," she said proudly and explained about the live shot at the hospital. He didn't seem pleased, nor displeased. His expression remained the same. "Is something wrong?" she asked.

"No, everything's fine," he said. "That's good news."

❧

"That's good news," Tyler said again as he heard a repeat of the quintuplet story from Tim. But it was not good news. The nation was about to see Kate Malone, and he predicted the viewers would fall in love with her, just as he had. He closed his eyes at that thought, but he'd wrestled with it all yesterday and come to the solid conclusion that he loved her. He didn't know her well, but each new bit of information he learned about her convinced him that he wanted to spend the rest of his life learning more and more. If there were such a thing as love at first sight, then he had it.

He'd seen her on screen, but that first glimpse of the real Kate Malone at the post office was etched in his mind. His heart had pounded when he saw her, and it had not slowed down since. Maybe she *had* given his grandmother a stroke; she might be giving him one.

He was in a foul mood. He'd been working behind the scenes with Mike Dodd, the evening news producer, to line up interviews with weathermen. This morning he'd had Richard fire his nephew, the noon weatherman, and now he was going to fire Richard. This station couldn't compete with others in the weather department. He'd have to invest a bundle to get the Doppler radar system they needed, and that should have been a need Richard had foreseen.

Tyler had been over at Channel 8 in Evansville, Indiana, and seen their system. Incredible. They could track a tornado down to the square block. It was spring now, tornado season in Kentucky. He had some personnel looking into systems and analyzing which would be best for WKYS, but if they could get a system ordered tomorrow, it wouldn't be installed and ready for several weeks.

This station had been the most neglected of any of Sinclair holdings, and it was, time it was treated right. There was money in advertising, and that was what could make or break a station. At least the newsroom had computers, but he'd discovered they had been purchased just six months ago. Until then, John Yeager said they had used typewriters and had taped news story pages together on a conveyer belt and a reporter had turned the prompter for the anchors to read. If they'd had that system when Kate had applied for a job, he doubted she would have come to their station.

*Kate. Kate. Kate.* She occupied his thoughts, and he had to make some decisions about her. Of course, they might be taken out of his hands tomorrow after she made her network debut.

Tonight was a start. He'd not been able to avoid more calls from Susan Appleby and was taking her to dinner tonight to break off their relationship, although the relationship was mostly in her mind. They'd gone together to a few charity functions since he'd returned to Bend, but for him she had been a convenience date. Now he wanted to be free of any obligations that relationship carried. He'd opted for the plush French Hen for dinner. Susan liked that type of opulence, so it should soften the blow.

Mike Dodd was in the newsroom and looked at him with a question in his eyes. Tyler nodded and marched to Richard's office. Mike would take over as station manager on a trial basis as soon as Richard was gone, which should be in half an hour. Tyler had a severance paycheck in his coat pocket and also had insurance information. Sinclair's personnel office had been thorough in going through the legal steps necessary for letting someone go. They even had a cleaning crew standing by to polish that office to a glow as soon as Richard vacated it.

It wasn't as bad as Tyler had thought it would be. Richard must have seen it coming after having to fire his nephew. The two o'clock meeting with the evening news staff was delayed only half an hour, but of course, the station had buzzed with the news before then. Richard didn't say good-bye to the people he had worked with; he merely loaded a couple boxes with personal belongings and walked out the back door.

Tyler turned down the volume on that tiresome scanner and called the meeting to order, then waited a moment as Kate hurried into the station and took her chair.

"Changes are underway at WKYS," Tyler said. "As of now, Mike Dodd is acting station manager. He'll also be producing the evening news, so he's going to need cooperation from everyone. He'll be interviewing people for producer, so if any of you want to apply, do so before we advertise the job in trade journals.

"Our weather center is undergoing a major overhaul. Channel 8 won't be the only one with dual Doppler radar. We want to be a full-service TV station. We don't want viewers to watch our news then switch to Channel 8 for the weather forecast.

"We're setting a target date of May 1 for a new set, new weather center, new sports corner, and by then the anchors will be wearing street clothes instead of station jackets. We'll be hyping the news debut with ads on screen and in the newspapers. To make all this happen at once, we're going to need everyone's help."

"Isn't that awfully fast?" Debra asked.

"Sweeps month is May. No better time to show a new improved WKYS," he said. "You may be asked to do more than your own job until we get the station running smoothly."

"It'll be like during the flu epidemic," Tim piped in. "We can do it."

Reporters and anchors murmured in agreement.

"Congratulations to Kate for the network spot we'll be getting tomorrow. Let's make the most of it and show the big guys that they can call on WKYS anytime for national coverage."

Tyler glanced down the hall as the cleaning crew carried shiny green plants into the station manager's office. It was handy that Sinclair Corporation owned a florist wholesaler. When Mike Dodd walked into that office, it would be a new start for the station.

"Okay, Mike, I'll let you run the show." Tyler took a chair and Mike stood and talked about the entire news team working together. Tim spoke about assignments, and the meeting adjourned. Reporters went different directions as they prepared for the six o'clock news.

Tyler remained seated within earshot as Mike and Kate went over the necessary arrangements for tomorrow's live broadcast.

"Everything's cleared at the hospital," she said. "Zip can shoot from a doorway into the nursery, so we can get a picture of the babies."

Kate's eyes glowed with the excitement of her chance at a national audience. He couldn't blame her. At one time he'd been as excited about his career plan for the Pentagon. That seemed a lifetime ago instead of less than a year. No, he couldn't blame her.

"I'm going back to the office," he told Mike. "Good luck tomorrow, Kate. I'll be watching." He wanted to say more, but it wouldn't be professional to plead with her not to do the remote shot tomorrow. It wouldn't be professional to kiss her in front of all the others, either. "See you later," he said and walked out.

The day dragged on with one problem to solve after another. He watched the six o'clock news while he changed clothes, and then he left to pick up Susan.

She was a beautiful woman. There was no doubt about that. She was bright and witty, but there was absolutely no spark between them.

Susan chatted on as he drove to the French Hen. He'd wait until dessert to tell her he wasn't interested in a dating relationship. She'd say something like that was fine and that they would always be friends, in her sophisticated way, and then he'd take her home. End of story. At least, he hoped it would go that smoothly.

The maitre d' seated them immediately, and a waiter brought water and menus. Tyler perused the choices and ordered for the two of them. He might as well enjoy the evening. Susan was always attentive and good for a man's ego. He smiled at her and then froze. Across the room, the maitre d' was seating Kate Malone, and she wasn't alone. The man with her looked several years older than Kate—was probably his own age, maybe older.

She was laughing up at him, and he teasingly reached down and flipped her hair before taking his chair. This was no business dinner. This was not an advertiser who wanted to talk to the female anchor. This was someone she knew and knew quite well.

She must have felt his gaze, for she looked his way, and for an instant he thought he saw panic or alarm in her eyes before she lifted a hand in a wave and smiled at him.

Perhaps he had been premature in deciding to break off with Susan. He'd thought since he felt so strongly about Kate that she also felt that way about him. She'd certainly kissed him back Saturday night. And they hadn't stopped at one kiss. One had led to another and another until she had told him that he'd better go.

Tyler tried to focus his attention on Susan, but his gaze strayed time and again to Kate and her dinner companion. He choked down the rich French food, which should have been the best in town, but it could have been sawdust for all he noticed.

At least he was with a woman. Kate wasn't the only one with another date. What if he and Joel had come here? But that would never happen. This was a couples' restaurant. All around him, even on a Monday night, couples dined, looking fondly over the table at each other.

The evening wore on. Why wasn't she at work? He ought to march over there and order her back to the station. But what would that prove—that he was insanely jealous and couldn't stand the thought of her being with another man?

Dessert, some strawberry concoction that Susan wanted, was served. Now was the time he had planned to tell her that he wasn't going to date her anymore, but he didn't say a word.

"What is it, Tyler? Bad day at the office? You've said three words all evening, and you haven't paid a bit of attention to what I've said, either."

He shook his head. "Sorry. I have a lot on my mind." His gaze darted involuntarily to Kate.

Susan turned in her chair and looked behind her. "Isn't that the news anchor?"

"Yes, it is. She should be at work," he said brusquely.

Susan laughed. "So, you have personnel problems."

"Actually we *are* undergoing a restructuring at the station. Major changes. We have a new station manager as of today."

"So that explains your mood. Really, Tyler, you should try to relax more, not take your work home with you."

"You're probably right," he said. He glanced at Kate's table. Her date was signing a credit card slip, and they were getting ready to leave. He was going to confront her now, demand an introduction, and tap down this feeling of betrayal. "Are you ready?"

"No coffee?"

"Perhaps at your place," he said and stood up. He motioned to the waiter and pulled some large bills out of his pocket. He left an overgenerous tip, because he didn't want to wait for change, and ushered Susan to the entrance where Kate's date was helping her with a light coat.

"Hello, Kate," he said. "I'm surprised to see you here." He looked pointedly at the man by her side. There was something familiar about him, but he couldn't place where he might have met him before.

"Good evening, Tyler," she said in a cool voice. "I'd like you to meet Harold. This is the owner of the station, Tyler Sinclair."

"Harold Malone," the man said and held out his hand.

"Malone? You're related to Kate?" Tyler tried to keep the relief out of his voice as he shook hands. The resemblance was there, all right. It was in the eyes.

"Her oldest brother," Harold said.

"Harold's visiting from Oregon," Kate said and glanced at Susan.

Tyler introduced his date. "She's very active on several charity boards I'm on." He hoped that information would make Kate understand that there wasn't a relationship between them.

Susan must have gotten the message, for she frowned and slipped her hand on Tyler's arm. "Nice to meet you," she said. "Weren't we going to my place for coffee, Tyler?"

He didn't answer but instead looked at Kate. "What time will you be at the hospital tomorrow morning?"

"Five-thirty."

"I'll see you then," he said and opened the door for Susan. He was suddenly anxious to get to Susan's home and break off the relationship.

# ten

As Kate drove to the hospital, she played yesterday's shake-up events in her mind like a video. First, the wonderful call from the network wanting her to interview the quints' parents on live TV. If her brother hadn't been coming to dinner, she would never have gone in early and gotten that plumb assignment. She'd discovered that Debra would go to any limit to get a news story for herself, and Kate wouldn't trust her again.

Next, Tyler had called the afternoon meeting to order, which was quite irregular. With military punctiliousness, he'd told them that Richard was gone and Mike Dodd was the new station manager. She was pleased with the reorganization. Mike cared about the station. It wasn't just a job to him.

And finally, the fiasco of last night's dinner with Harold. Oh, the food had been exquisite, she thought, but she couldn't remember the taste. What she remembered was Tyler sitting across the room with Susan Appleby. She had never felt such betrayal in her life. Over what? A few kisses on Saturday night? A feeling of such rightness when she was with Tyler? A connected feeling?

She had purposefully not given Harold's last name when she'd introduced him to Tyler, but Harold hadn't gotten the hint and had blurted it out. She'd wanted Tyler to think that she had a date, too.

"So, what's between you two?" Harold had asked on the way back to the station. "Tyler was obviously relieved to know I was your brother."

"I doubt that. I guarantee that wasn't his sister with him. And there's nothing between us," she'd said with vehemence.

130

Harold had laughed. "Even when you were little, I could always tell when you were lying. You get this furtive look in your eyes and your forehead wrinkles."

Kate had glanced at the rearview mirror and seen the wrinkles he'd described. They were there now, too, she noticed with a quick glance in the mirror as she changed lanes to turn into the hospital parking lot. But this time they were from apprehension.

"Dear God, please help me with this interview," she prayed aloud. "It's important to the station that I do well, and it's important to me. And please let me put Tyler Sinclair out of my mind."

She pulled the car into the parking place next to a car with WKYS emblazoned on it. On the other side of it was Tyler's Lincoln. "I guess avoiding Tyler isn't in Your plan, is it, God? Are You teaching me something through this?" She nodded in resignation. "Your will be done."

She walked with purpose toward the entrance to the hospital and took the stairs to obstetrics. The halls were quiet at this early hour, and she walked softly to muffle the click-click of her heels.

She turned the corner toward the nursery and found a charged atmosphere. Zip stood behind the camera, checking light meters and angles. The satellite feed was already hooked up and ready. Tyler, in a business suit, visited quietly with the main doctor who had delivered the quints.

Tyler looked straight at Kate and nodded a greeting, then turned his attention back to the doctor.

"The C-section went perfectly. Those babies were born only seconds apart. They seemed eager to come into the world."

That was the type of quote she'd gotten from him yesterday. Each person had told of his view of the births, and remarkably there had been little repetition. The network would use the footage from yesterday's interviews, along with an update from the nursery where the mother and father would be holding the infants.

Kate spoke briefly with Zip about the shot, then walked down the hall to Ginger Brett's room. The new mother was awake and fiddling with her hair.

"Let me do that," Kate said. She cranked up the bed and brushed Ginger's hair away from her face. "How are you feeling? Are you up to doing this?"

"I feel all right," Ginger said. "Had pain medicine at four, so I wouldn't be too groggy. I'm still tired. What I really feel is skinny. I spent the last two months in bed and looked like I'd swallowed a giant balloon. Now I want to get back to my normal self. With five babies to tend to, I should get back in shape in no time. I taught a night class in aerobics before I got pregnant."

"That's probably why you're doing so well."

"That and the good Lord wanting me healthy to take care of my babies. As soon as they all reach four pounds, we'll go home. They lose a little weight right off, then gain it back."

"Hey, save some of this stuff for the interview," Kate said. "I thought babies had to weigh five pounds before they were dismissed."

"Not anymore. The important thing is that all parts are functioning."

They talked a few more minutes while Kate helped Ginger with makeup. "You can't look too glamorous or they'll think we hired an actress to play the part," Kate said, and Ginger looked pleased.

Ginger's husband walked in the room and wheeled Ginger to the nursery while Kate pushed the IV pole alongside. They donned surgical gowns and Kate put the parents and the doctor in position and attached their microphones. She snapped one on herself and tested for volume. Out of the corner of her eye, she saw Tyler watching through the nursery windows. A TV had been placed in the hallway, so Kate could see the network morning show, which was already on the air. She adjusted the IFB in her ear, which would allow her to hear questions from New York.

"We're three minutes away. Would you two like to hold the babies?" she asked the parents. Nurses disconnected monitors and carried two infants to Ginger, one to her husband, and another to the doctor. A nurse handed the last baby girl to Kate, who was temporarily dumbfounded.

Sure, she was gowned so she could be in the nursery, but she hadn't anticipated holding such a tiny creature.

Zip held up his fingers, and Kate swallowed hard and glanced toward Tyler. Four-three-two-one. The TV in the hall showed footage from yesterday's interview then went to a split screen of Kate and the network host.

"Good morning, Kate Malone, at our affiliate in Bend, Kentucky. I see you have one of the remarkable infants in your arms."

"I can't believe I'm actually holding one of the day-old quintuplets. This is Melissa, the oldest of the sisters."

Kate didn't remember much else of what she said, but in the minute and a half allowed for her live segment, she asked questions of the parents and the doctor. Melissa whimpered, and Kate cooed softly, "It's all right, sweetie. It's all right," and Melissa settled down.

"All of America wishes the Brett family well. We'll be checking in on your daughters for periodic updates. Kate Malone of WKYS, you look like a natural with that infant. You may be called on to baby-sit," the host said with a chuckle. "Thank you for being with us," he added.

"My pleasure," Kate said, and Zip gave the all clear sign.

The hallway TV showed the station going to commercial. The satellite feed was still in place, and the host asked Kate through her earpiece if she'd cover the quints going home from the hospital.

"I'll arrange for it," Kate said, "and call you with details." Another network appearance. This kind of exposure could mean a shot at a bigger market. But was that what she wanted? She glanced at Tyler and decided it might be best if she moved on. She turned her attention back to the activity around her.

"Thank you for letting us do this," Kate told Ginger and her husband as the nurses took the babies back to incubators and hooked them to monitors. "It's a first to have such healthy babies with a multiple birth. I'm sure America hasn't seen day-old quints like this."

She was still amazed that the hospital had allowed a camera in the doorway to the nursery, and only WKYS's camera. Of course, Mount Carmel had been named, and that kind of publicity couldn't be bought. She asked about covering the quints leaving the hospital and got the Bretts' approval.

Kate collected microphones and helped Zip with the equipment. She kept herself occupied so that she didn't have to talk to Tyler, but soon everything was done, and she could delay the moment no longer.

"Good job, Kate," he said.

"Thanks. How's your grandmother doing?" she asked, but without waiting for an answer, continued. "I was wondering if you could ask her or find out from her address book the married name of Jane McFee. Remember Loren McFee, the author who was on the new stamp? He was a neighbor of your grandmother's when he was murdered forty years ago. I'm doing a series on unsolved murders, and I'd like to include him. An interview with his widow would really help the piece."

"I'll see what I can do," he said. "About last night. . ."

"Yes, the French Hen is quite a place, isn't it?" Kate said

brightly. She wasn't going to let on that she was in anyway hurt by Tyler having a date.

"Kate, did you set up a time for the next go-round?" Zip asked.

"I have the parents' okay, and I'd better catch the doctor now," she said and could have kissed Zip for the interruption. "Excuse me, Tyler."

"Sure. Oh, Kate," he said softly and pulled her aside so only she could hear. "It looks like good weather for our sail Saturday. Joel and Chelsea are going with us," he said. "I'll call you."

"Fine," she said. She had forgotten the sail that he'd bought at the Boys and Girls Club. Last night's reality check had erased their date from her mind. Should she break it? Her heart ached already just because she'd seen Tyler out with another woman. She had no ties on him. She had been on a total of two dates with him, if she counted the Sunday dinner with Jacob's family and the fund raiser. She hadn't even been out to a real restaurant dinner with him. Why did she think he would be seeing only her? It was those church bells that she'd heard when she first saw him. Well, that was only fanciful thinking. It was no message from God; it was coincidence. She'd better start thinking practically. And right now that meant getting on with this assignment. She excused herself by saying, "I'll talk to you later," and scurried after the doctor.

Instead of going home after the shoot, Kate headed to the station. She was already dressed, ready for the day, and Mike might need help. She was ready to pitch in and do her share to help the station run smoothly during the transition time.

"Anyone put in his application for producer?" she asked Mike.

"Not yet. You interested?"

"No. Just wondered. I thought Tim might want that spot."

"Me, too. I'll talk to him. Hey, we've had tons of requests for our footage of the quints. Imagine us with exclusive coverage."

Kate could hardly imagine it. She was sure there would be lots of cameras outside the hospital when the quints left, but at least theirs was the only one allowed inside. Knowing when the quints would be dismissed was a hard call, since it depended on weight gain, but a week was anticipated.

Kate turned her thoughts to her other stories and called Rocky, the retired police detective, who told her he was working on a few leads about the illusive Mrs. McFee. Kate told him she was working on it, too, and wondered if Tyler would remember to ask his grandmother about her friend.

❧

Tyler pulled under the portico of the Sinclair mansion on the hill overlooking the city. Kate hadn't let him explain about Susan Appleby, although he guessed there really wasn't a need. He was acting solely on his idea of the Golden Rule. He was treating Kate the way he wanted to be treated, and that was to know if the person she was with had special meaning to her. Wouldn't she want to know the same about him? But again, that was assuming that she was as interested in him as he was in her. She was, he was certain of it. But then, why wasn't she acting interested? When he'd reminded her of Saturday's date, she'd been momentarily taken aback, as if she'd forgotten. If he had to remind her of a date, then she wasn't interested at all, was she?

He shook his head to clear his muddled mind. That's what Kate did to him. She'd shaken up his world, and he liked it ordered, with him in charge. He should have gone straight to the office. He had enough to do since he'd been hanging around the station so much the last week. But since it wasn't yet eight, he'd decided to talk to Grandmother about Mrs. McFee. The name stirred a vague memory, but maybe that was because the stamp story had lodged in his mind. He hadn't even been born forty years ago when McFee had been murdered.

With Mrs. McFee's married name in hand, he had a good reason to call Kate and be on a professional basis, if that's what she wanted. He just wished he knew what she wanted. Why wasn't she as straight with him as Susan Appleby? Susan would have gladly become Mrs. Tyler Sinclair. She'd made no secret of it, and last night she'd accused him of leading her on, although he didn't think he was guilty. The breaking-off scenario hadn't gone as well as he'd thought it would. Maybe if he'd done it at the restaurant instead of at her apartment, she would have reacted differently. Not so demonstratively. At least it was finished.

He wandered into the house and to the breakfast room at the back. Mother was lingering over coffee. Grandmother wasn't there.

Tyler kissed his mother on the cheek and poured himself a cup from the pot on the buffet.

"I saw Kate Malone this morning. She did very well. Seemed quite comfortable in front of millions of viewers."

"But she was only in front of a handful of us," Tyler said. "Whether local or national, she's talking to a camera."

"True. But a lot of people would let that intimidate them. Kate Malone crooned to that baby just like she was in her own living room. That's what the big broadcasters do. Katie Couric, Jane Pauley, Lisa McRee. They all talk to the camera like they're talking to a friend over the kitchen table."

Tyler knew she was right. Kate Malone had *it*. That undefinable something. Presence. Poise. Assurance. Confidence. All rolled together.

"She may be headed up, but we've got her right now. She signed a six-month contract." He'd looked in her file. He had a little over four months to convince her that this was the place to stay. Or was it less time than that? Could she already be sending out her tape, allowing for interview time? She'd probably give a month's notice. And a month prior to that she'd be deciding where she wanted to go. Make it two months he had to persuade her to stay in Bend, Kentucky.

"How's Grandmother doing? Is she up?"

"She's better today. She's gotten in the habit of eating breakfast in bed. I don't think it's necessary, but she's found it relaxing. Your grandmother's been a mover-and-shaker for a long time. I think she's finally beginning to see things from a distance instead of from in the middle of the fray."

"That won't last long. She'll want in the action as soon as her speech is back to normal. It will improve, won't it?"

"You'll notice an improvement today. Yesterday seemed to be a turning point. Go on in and talk to her."

Tyler carried his coffee cup with him and knocked on Grandmother's door. She called, "Come in," and he easily understood her.

"Grandmother, how are you?" he asked and stooped and kissed her. She was propped up in the bed with several pillows behind her, the TV news show on across the room, and a bed tray with legs over her lap. Her plate and juice glass were empty. She poured herself a cup of coffee with one hand and picked up the coffee in the same hand. She still didn't have full usage of one side.

"Getting better," she said, and although it was recognizable, it wasn't her normal tone and diction.

Tyler exchanged pleasantries with the old woman, then asked about Mrs. McFee.

A look of fear crossed her face and was quickly replaced by a determined countenance.

"Why?" she barked the word.

He explained about Kate's series.

"That was forty years ago. People aren't interested in that, but it's nothing to me. Jane McFee married Thomas Horance a couple years after Loren was killed, but I think they divorced and she married someone else. I can't remember."

She was talking fast, and her speech was getting more and more garbled. He half suspected she was talking fast on purpose.

"Just thought I'd ask. Well, I'd better get to work." He filled her in on the changes at WKYS, and she nodded as if she agreed with his business decisions. He kissed her good-bye and left for the office.

Something wasn't right with Grandmother and the McFee thing. He searched his mind during his drive to the office, and by the time the elevator doors opened on the tenth floor, he remembered. That time that Grandmother had been so furious when the library had named a reading room after some writer—Loren McFee had been the honoree. Grandmother had spent the weekend throwing a tantrum and had never set foot in the building again.

Tyler frowned. Kate was right to tackle that murder from this end. His grandmother knew something, but he wasn't sure what. Well, he could tell Kate the name, but he doubted it would help her.

He called her duplex, but the answering machine picked up, and he didn't leave a message. Instead, he punched in the number of the station.

"Kate," he said when she came on the line, "I have a lead for you, but it's probably not going to help with your McFee murder." He told her what his grandmother had said about Jane McFee. Kate sounded all professional, not at all like the woman he had held in his arms on Saturday night.

"I appreciate your help, Tyler. I'll see if I can go anywhere with that name."

"About Saturday. We're to have lunch on board the sail-boat, so I'll pick you up around ten."

"That sounds fine. I'll see you then," Kate said. "And thanks for the information. I have another call, so I'll talk to you later."

Another call. She'd probably have many calls that day, some from other stations. Wasn't that how it worked in the TV business? Tyler hung up the phone with more force than necessary.

≈

Kate was unprepared for the response to her network premier. The entire segment with her taped session and the live portion that morning could have run only two and a half minutes. Her family called and were properly impressed, but it was the professional calls that amazed her. She'd had an on-the-spot offer from a station in Denver. Of course, she'd told them she was under contract, but the lure tugged at her mind all day as she worked on other stories for the six o'clock news.

Her move to Bend had been carefully planned. It was a step up in broadcasting, and it was a step closer to family. What was important to her? She couldn't discount a career. She'd worked hard to get where she was now, but was it where she wanted to be? On the broadcast journalism success scale, she was perched on about the fifth rung of a ten-story ladder. Was she content to stay there? This move to Bend had been a search for her place in life. She had listed pros and cons before moving to Kentucky and thought she might find what would make her happy. She didn't want to hit the top. She didn't want the type of life someone like Oprah had. That woman couldn't even go to the grocery store without being mobbed. Someone had to do her shopping for her.

As it was, Kate usually shopped after work at night. She'd learned in Rochester that people were curious about TV personnel. They didn't consider it a violation of privacy to look in her shopping cart to see what she was buying. And she was very small potatoes compared to someone in a big market.

She mulled the situation over in her mind, but was no closer to a decision when she went on the air at six. A few minutes after the early news had ended, the call came in about a major fire in a deserted downtown building. Reporters were on assignment or had gone off work, but Kate hadn't left for supper yet, so Mike sent her to get film for the ten o'clock slot.

By the time Kate arrived with camera in tow, the fire had spread to the buildings on both sides. Half an hour later the entire block was ablaze, and the incredible heat from the fire forced her to move farther and farther back and use all the power of her telephoto lenses.

Kate dialed the station on her cell phone and asked Mike for the remote van. If she stayed on the scene, John Yeager would have to read the news alone, but the story of the hour was here. She filmed interviews with the fire chief and a policeman. A man who owned the hardware store that was going up in flames spoke to her in an emotion-choked voice. These videos would be broadcast from the van.

Moments before she was to go live from the scene at ten, firemen found a body pressed against a locked door in the empty building. They carried the lifeless man out into the street and covered him with a tarp, but not before Kate saw his charred face.

She stifled a sob and turned inside herself for the strength to do her job. "God, help me," she murmured. It was as if she detached herself from the scene and gave the who, what, where, when, why, and how of the story and answered John Yeager's questions as he spoke to her through her earpiece. When her first segment was over, she slipped into the shadows and retched.

"You all right?" The remote operator came up behind her.

"I've never seen anything like that," Kate said. In her early days as a reporter, she'd covered horrible car wrecks and learned to distance herself from emotion, but it had taken a while to develop the necessary hardness. She struggled to find that professional core again. "John will close with us, so we'd better get ready. Mike wants special bulletins over the next couple hours." She walked on unsteady legs to the front of the van.

"Hey, Kate."

She recognized Dale Webster of competing Channel 8 from Evansville, Indiana. They'd met at other events where area stations had covered the same story.

"Got any extra batteries?" he asked. "Mine are dead."

"Sure." She found a couple of charged batteries in her camera case and gave them to Dale. Some reporters didn't believe in giving the competition help, but as in the rest of her life, Kate evoked the Golden Rule and treated Dale like she'd want to be treated if she were in that situation.

"Thanks. I owe you," Dale said. "It's a horrible fire. Did you hear about the fatality?"

"Yes," she said in a small voice.

"We're closing in three," the remote operator said.

Kate adjusted her earpiece and positioned herself with the worst of the fire as the backdrop.

She watched the small screen as John Yeager gave the lead into the fire, then switched to her. She couldn't keep an emotional edge out of her voice as she recounted the events and mentioned there had been at least one death.

"Is that fatality confirmed officially?" John asked.

"Official, no. Confirmed, yes. I saw it," Kate said in her tough news voice, but wiped away a tear. "The body was burned beyond recognition. We'll have updates on the fire later in the evening."

It was when she laid down the mike that she saw Tyler standing at the side of the van.

She couldn't stop herself. She ran straight into his arms and sobbed and sobbed.

## eleven

"It's all right," Tyler murmured in her ear as he held her tightly. "It's all right." She had a death grip around his neck, but he welcomed it. The anguish in her eyes when she had appeared at ten o'clock with the top story had compelled him to hurry downtown. It had taken time to find her. Streets were cordoned off, and he'd had to park eight blocks away. When he'd spotted the remote van's high antenna pole, he'd zeroed in on that spot and arrived just in time to see her give batteries to a reporter and take her position for the news. He'd stayed behind the van to watch, but the moment she had gone off the air, he'd stepped into her line of sight.

After her cool, professional treatment that morning and later on the phone, he was surprised by the way she had thrown herself at him. She had reached her limit and needed to be held. Death did that to people. It made them want to be near living, breathing human beings. He'd seen it when he'd been in the Middle East and when he'd been in Oklahoma City after the bombing there. No matter the location or culture, it was the same reaction.

"It's all right," he said in her ear. Her sobs were subsiding little by little, and within a few minutes, she drew away from him.

"I'm sorry," she said. "I just feel so safe with you."

"Good," he said. "I feel safe with you."

She looked into his eyes, and he felt she was looking into his soul and seeing his love for her.

"I must get back to work. We're going to update the story every half-hour."

While she roamed with a camera and a mike, Tyler walked to Shorty's restaurant and picked up barbecue sandwiches and coffee and carried them back to the remote van. Kate had finished the eleven o'clock update and was on the phone with Mike Dodd. As soon as she disconnected, she and the remote operator devoured the food.

"I didn't get to eat supper," she said. "Thanks."

"How long will you stay here?" Tyler asked.

"Mike says we'll shut down at midnight. Not many viewers will hang on after that. If they're that interested, they'd be down here."

Although firemen trained hoses on the fire, they didn't seem to have an effect on the flames.

"They're trying to contain the fire to this block. I heard they're soaking buildings on the back side of the block, but the fire has already jumped the alley. I'd better get some footage of that."

Tyler carried her camera and together they made a wide circle of the fire-consumed area and came out on the far side. The night sky was lit up flame-red, and dark smoke roiled out of broken windows.

"That one's on fire," Tyler said and pointed to the top of a six-story building.

Kate captured it on film, then they scurried back to the remote van to give an update.

Adrenaline surged through Tyler. The feeling matched the one he felt when he was high in the air in a fighter plane, but that was a dim memory now. So this was what Kate Malone, newswoman, felt when she was in the midst of a story. He doubted that many of her stories held this much excitement or danger. He hoped not.

His original plans for the TV station had included following a reporter around all day to get a taste of what the job was like, just as he'd gone on a three-day haul with a trucker when he'd studied the trucking firm. But he hadn't planned on a long day like this one. He had met Kate that morning at the hospital at five-thirty, and here it was nearly midnight, and they were still going.

After Mike Dodd called the news team to the station, Tyler followed in his car and helped unload equipment.

"I'll see you home," he told Kate.

"No need. I'm all right," Kate said.

"It's on my way." He followed her car, parked in her driveway, and walked her to the door. He wanted one kiss, one solitary kiss to carry him through the night. He pulled her in his arms, their lips met for a moment, then they leaned heavily on each other.

Holding her like this was better than the brief kiss they'd just shared.

"I'd better go in," she said. "I'm so tired."

"I know. Sleep well, Kate." He gave her one more kiss, then turned and left.

⁂

The shrill ringing of the phone woke Kate a little after seven.

"Turn on Channel 8 at 7:25 when they run the local report," Chelsea said without preamble.

"Channel 8? Why are you watching the competition?" Kate stretched for the remote control on the night stand and clicked on the bedroom TV.

"I watched Leno last night, so that's the channel that came on when I tuned in this morning, and guess who I saw on the screen?"

Kate searched her mind. Channel 8. "Dale Webster? He covered the fire last night. Is it under control? Do we have someone down there now?"

She flipped to WKYS, but the network morning show was on. The cutaway to local news was at 7:25, same as on Channel 8.

"There was more than one fire last night. And the one downtown is under control. I'm not sure about the other one. Channel 8 has an exclusive."

"I'm still fuzzy from exhaustion," Kate said. "There was another fire last night? Was it purposefully set?"

"Definitely purposefully set. I'll say no more. Just watch Channel 8," Chelsea said and hung up.

Now that she was wide awake, Kate made a pot of coffee and propped herself up in bed to watch the morning show. She wanted to watch her own station to see how last night's footage had been edited for this morning's news, but she dutifully stayed on Channel 8.

Of course, the top news story was the fire. As she watched the film of the burning buildings, Kate was transported to last night and the intensity of the blaze. The footage showed the fire, then turned to the crowd who watched. There in the bright flickering light from the fire stood Tyler Sinclair holding Kate Malone. A close-up showed him kissing her hair and mouthing something as he held her. She could read his lips. "It's all right."

She remembered saying those words to one of the quint infants yesterday morning. Tyler had soothed her the same way.

The camera panned others in the crowd, then coverage turned to this morning's charred remains of that downtown block.

Kate grabbed the phone on the first ring.

"Did you see it? I knew they'd show it again," Chelsea said.

"I lent him the batteries for that shot, and I never even got them back. Dale Webster is in big trouble."

"Actually, I think you're in big trouble. Until now, I was the only one who knew there was something between you and the boss. Now it's going to be common knowledge."

"Maybe no one else is watching the competition," Kate said, but knew the TVs in the newsroom were tuned to the three area stations.

"Ha!" Chelsea said. "Hey, I'm looking forward to going sailing Saturday. I guess I can see the second fire firsthand then."

"It's not what it seems," Kate said. "It was very emotional at the fire. And I badly needed comforting. You might as well know, Chelsea. Uh," Kate stalled. She didn't know how to say it. "Tyler's seeing someone." There she'd put it into words, and she didn't like the sound of them.

"Isn't he seeing you?"

"I guess, since we have that date Saturday, but he could have several others on the string for all I know." Kate told her about Susan Appleby. "So, now you know. Tyler and I are sort of business acquaintances."

"Didn't look much like business on the news. I think all the facts aren't in. I'll do some investigating reporting."

"Don't you dare ask Joel if Tyler likes me and all that fifth-grade stuff. Please, Chelsea, just leave it alone. We'll have a good time on the sail, and that will be that. I've got to get around. See you at the station."

She couldn't talk any more. She'd been angry and she'd been hurt, and now the tears fell. She slipped a tape in her VCR, and when Channel 8 gave the local news at seven-fifty-five, she recorded it. True to form, they repeated the same footage. At WKYS they had a policy of taking tons of footage. Even if they repeated the top stories, they showed different video so the viewers wouldn't switch channels. This time she was glad that Channel 8 took the easy way. She watched the video several times and froze the frame when Tyler kissed her hair.

"Think logically," she said aloud. Was this just a moment of comfort or was there something more? "God," she prayed,

"I don't know what to think. I'm turned inside out and upside down. Please show me the way."

She put the tape away, showered, and dressed. She called Rocky and asked if he could put her on the trail of anyone to talk to on the other two unsolved murders in her series. She'd neglected them since her interest lay in the McFee murder. She wrote down the names he mentioned and gave him Jane McFee's second husband's name.

That afternoon she'd just arrived at the station when Rocky called her.

"That wasn't hard," he said. "Her ex-husband was glad to tell me that Jane McFee Horance Lauderback lives a two-hour drive from here in Elm Grove, Illinois. Want to go with me to talk to her?"

Kate checked her schedule. It was too late to make the trip today and be back for the news. "Is tomorrow good for you?" she asked. "Early? I can get a station car. Should we let her know we're coming or surprise her?"

"Surprise is always best in cases like this," he said. "I'll meet you at your station at seven."

Kate checked with Tim and arranged for a car. "I probably won't be back for the afternoon meeting," she said.

"That's all right," he said. "This afternoon's meeting is more important. Sinclair will be here at two and wants to talk about the new set. By the way, we've all seen Channel 8's coverage. What's going on with you two?"

"Nothing really. We're just friends. Last night he was there right after the body had been discovered. I was a little upset."

"Body still hasn't been identified, but police think it was an indigent in that vacant building. Probably got lost in the smoke and couldn't find his way out. An autopsy is scheduled."

Kate didn't want to think about the poor soul who had been trapped in that building, so she turned her thoughts elsewhere as she'd trained herself to do. It felt heartless, but she pulled a professional cloak around her and looked at the stories scheduled for six. She'd think about the poor man later. Now all she could do was murmur "God rest his soul," and move on.

She had reviewed the fire tapes for a clip to run that night with the follow-up story. Debra had interviewed property owners and gotten footage of the charred remains. It was old news, but it was big news, and viewers would tune in again to see it at six and ten.

The fire also reminded her of Dale Webster. She looked up the number and called Channel 8.

"You owe me two batteries," she said as soon as she'd identified herself, "and an apology."

"Hey, I figure Tyler Sinclair is news. He avoids the press, and there he was in plain sight hugging a news anchor. You would have shot it, too."

"Maybe," Kate admitted, then added thoughtfully, "and maybe not."

"Want a tape of it?"

"No, I recorded it," she said.

Dale Webster laughed. "I'll drop off those two batteries, all charged and ready to go, when I get off work. See you."

Their short conversation had Kate wondering if she would have taped a member of the Sinclair family in a private moment. Okay, Dale was scanning the crowd, but he had focused on Tyler. He'd done it specifically because he was Tyler Sinclair. Did that have the sting of tabloid reporting? Was she guilty of the same thing when she'd taped that dog story?

No. She was filming a Good Samaritan story, not focusing on someone because his name would make the news. Where would she draw the line? What was news and what was invasion of privacy? Sure, she and Tyler had been in public last night for anyone to see, but the moment was purely one of comfort needed and comfort given. Taken out of context, it gave a different impression than what was really true. Didn't it?

She went through the motions of reading the news stories that were already finished, but her mind wasn't on the content. It was on Tyler Sinclair, and then the man himself walked in the side door.

Mike Dodd whistled to get the attention of everyone in the newsroom. Someone turned down the scanner, and the afternoon meeting was in session. Tyler smiled at Kate, but then he focused on Mike, who went through the usual business and then let Tyler speak.

There were humorous glances at Kate as Tyler stood. He glanced her way, too, with a quizzical look in his eye. So, he hadn't seen Channel 8's picture of them together. She supposed she should tell him after the meeting.

Tyler spoke about more changes coming to the station. He reviewed the suggestions for the new sets and asked for discussion.

Consensus was to have three distinct sets for the noon, six, and ten o'clock news. The station logo would be the backdrop for the noon news. The newsroom itself would be the backdrop for the six o'clock. "Minus that constant chatter," Tyler said and pointed at the scanner. The ten o'clock would use a giant photo of the skyline of Bend, as if the news crew were sitting in front of a window.

With that decided, Mike Dodd dismissed the meeting, and the normal din of six conversations going on at once returned.

"How are you?" Tyler asked as he stood by Kate's desk. "Have you recuperated from yesterday's full day?"

"I'm okay. Uh. . .uh," she stuttered around, trying to find the words to tell him what had been on Channel 8. Finally she just blurted it out.

"So that's why I've had a few odd looks today," he said, but he didn't seem upset by it. "They all want me to think that they watch our station, so no one told me. As long as

Grandmother didn't see it—and she never watches any other station—it doesn't matter."

"It doesn't bother you to be associated with me like that?" Kate asked.

He looked long and hard at her. "Of course not."

Kate wondered what Susan Appleby would have to say if she saw that video, but she didn't ask. Tyler left her area to meet with Mike Dodd, then he returned right before he left for his office, telling her in a low voice that he was looking forward to their sail.

For once Kate wished she didn't work nights. She couldn't have a normal relationship of a pizza and a movie during mid-week. Her social life was confined to weekends, but she did have a date this Saturday.

The next morning, Kate arrived at the station by six-thirty and loaded equipment into a station hatchback. Rocky was early, and they took off for Elm Grove and pulled into Jane McFee's driveway shortly before nine. There was no answer when Kate rang the doorbell.

"That's the one problem with the element of surprise," Rocky said. "Sometimes you have to stake out." He paced the front porch that ran the length of the front of the older home.

"Are you wanting the Lauderbacks?" A woman on the other side of a hedge called.

"Yes," Kate answered. "Do you know when they'll be back?"

"Monday afternoon on the two o'clock flight. Jane and Ralph have been visiting his daughter in Colorado. I'm taking care of their place. Why do you want them?" She motioned to the car emblazoned with WKYS on the side. "Aren't you Kate Malone? We get the Bend station on cable."

Kate introduced Rocky and shook hands with the neighbor, Mrs. Browne.

"We're doing 'man on the street' interviews in the towns that get our station," Rocky said. "Do you watch our station regularly?" He rattled off a few more standard questions that would be on any TV marketing survey.

Kate followed Rocky's cue and retrieved the camera and tripod and interviewed Mrs. Browne about the station and what she liked and what she didn't.

"This is for a promo shot," Kate said, and made a mental note to pursue this with Mike Dodd, so she wouldn't be a liar. "Would you mind if we lifted a quote from what you've said? It would be on why you like the station, of course."

"Why, that'd be fine," Mrs. Browne said.

After they'd loaded up the equipment, Kate drove them out of town and back onto the highway headed toward Bend.

"Let's come back early Tuesday morning," Rocky said.

"I think our element of surprise is gone. Mrs. Browne will surely tell the Lauderbacks we were there."

"Probably, but I think we covered all right. She never knew who I was, and I'm the only one Jane McFee might know."

They arranged for the same scenario on Tuesday. "This time I'm going to have some definite questions," Kate said. "Only when I was pushing that doorbell did I realize how ill-prepared I was to pin her down about the murder."

Kate was in plenty of time for the regular afternoon meeting, but Tyler wasn't there. Nor did he come to the station that day. Kate taped an update segment on the quintuplets for the network morning show, but the hospital dismissal date hadn't been set yet, so the live broadcast couldn't be scheduled.

❧

On Saturday morning, Kate dressed in white slacks and a navy short-sleeved top, perfect attire for a sail. As she waited for Tyler, she glanced out the front window. Clouds moved quickly across the sky. The Weather Channel gave a 40 percent chance of rain, but that was for Bend, and the lake was an hour's drive away. Who knew what it was doing there?

At ten, Tyler turned in the driveway. Kate could see Joel and Chelsea in the back seat of Tyler's Lincoln. She grabbed a windbreaker and met him at the door.

"What do you think?" she said and motioned to the sky.

"Hard to tell," he said and opened the passenger door for her. "We'll come up with something to do."

Joel and Chelsea were in high spirits, and Kate found herself carried away with the excitement of going on the lake and enjoying the camaraderie of the group. As the miles sped by, the clouds seemed to intensify. Tyler called their host on his cell phone, but there was no answer.

"He must already be there, getting things ready," Chelsea said, and her words proved true for they found the owner stowing provisions on the boat when they arrived at the lake.

They were standing on the dock, admiring the thirty-five-foot sailboat, when the first sprinkles hit the ground.

"Climb aboard," the owner said, and they scrambled on and climbed down into the cabin. The foursome sat at a booth-like table while the owner served them coffee.

"Beautiful boat," Kate said. This one was much larger than the one her friends sailed back home. The cabin seemed spacious, yet every inch had its function, and she examined it thoroughly from the galley with its alcohol stove to the berths in the bow, while the rain beat a steady rat-a-tat-tat on the deck over their heads. "Do you think it will let up?"

The owner shook his head. "It might be better to reschedule our sail. Nothing like a pretty day with a good breeze. We don't want to dodge lightning bolts on the lake."

"You're right," Tyler said, and they agreed to try it the following weekend. About twenty minutes later, when the rain let up some, the foursome made a dash for the car.

Kate shook water off her windbreaker before she slipped into the car. She bit back her disappointment. She loved the freedom that sailing made her feel, the challenge of taming the wind, and the sound of lapping water as the boat sliced through the waves.

She'd looked forward to this through the pressures of the past eventful days: learning that Tyler was seeing someone, going on the network show, covering the fire, and preparing for a confrontation with Jane McFee. This was to have been her reward for getting through stress-filled days. Now she wouldn't even get to spend time with Tyler.

She stared out the rain-streaked window at the passing farm lands as they sped along. Farmers called steady rain like this million-dollar rain, and the fields seemed to be greening up in front of her eyes. She turned her thoughts to the positive aspects of the rain instead of her disappointment.

"Okay," Tyler said. "We have a day ahead of us. Nothing like a rainy day for relaxing. Any ideas?"

"Let's start at your place," Joel suggested. "We can look at the paper and see what kind of action's in town."

The rain fell harder as they approached Bend. Tyler turned in his drive.

"Wow, this is some place," Chelsea said.

"It's lovely," Kate said. "It has such character." Even through the rain, the round brick columns that held up the second story balcony told her this house was very special.

Tyler parked in the circular drive as close to the front porch as he could manage, and they dashed for the house. He unlocked the door and ushered them inside.

"Want the fifty-cent tour?" he asked, then took them through the main floor of the house.

"This is my favorite room," Joel said when they were in the TV room with the big screen. They moved on to Tyler's office.

"I'm green with envy," Kate said as she admired the tall bookcases and the heavy oak desk. She read aloud the framed saying on the wall, "A quick-tempered man does foolish things. . ." She turned to Tyler. "Are you that quick-tempered man?"

Joel laughed. "I don't think that applies anymore. His mom gave him that after he joined the air force without telling them."

"Sounds like there's quite a story here," Kate said.

"Ancient history," Tyler said. "I've learned to think things through since then, although I don't regret joining the air force."

Kate looked down on the desk and saw the light blinking on his answering machine. "You have a message."

Tyler leaned over and pushed the button. "Hi, Tyler," a woman's sultry tones filled the room. Kate stiffened, and Joel said, "I'll show you the kitchen," and dragged Chelsea into the hall as Kate listened to Susan Appleby's message. "What did we decide about Saturday night? Give me a call."

Kate studied the carpeting, then lifted her head. "I'll join the others while you make your call," she said in a crisp voice. She took a step toward the door, but Tyler grabbed her hand and had her sit in the chair facing the desk. He shut the door, looked in his Rolodex, and punched in the number.

*At least he doesn't have her number programmed into his phone,* she thought.

"Susan, it's Tyler Sinclair. I thought we decided that you would work the early shift and get someone to cover from nine-thirty on." He scowled at the phone.

Kate studied book titles on the wall behind Tyler and hummed a song in her mind so she wouldn't strain to hear Susan's voice.

"I see. Well then, I'll take care of the late shift myself. Thanks for clearing that up. Good-bye."

He put down the receiver. "Are you under the impression that there is something between Susan and me? I tried to clear this up the other day at the hospital, but we got off on something else. Oh yes, you asked me to talk to Grandmother about the McFee case, so I figured you weren't disturbed by Susan. I was wrong, wasn't I?"

"I. . . Your love life is your business," Kate said.

"No, my love life is your business," Tyler said and strode around the desk and took Kate in his arms. "Susan has been an occasional date for community functions. That's all, and I took her out Monday night to explain that there was someone else in my life now."

"Someone else?"

"You, Kate. Aren't you in my life now?" He held her face still, mere inches from his own, and gazed into her eyes.

"Yes," she whispered and felt he had willed the admission from her. "Yes, I'm in your life."

And then he kissed her.

# twelve

As much as Kate liked sailing, it couldn't compare to Saturday at Tyler's house. In her mind she thanked God for the million-dollar rain that the farmers needed and the rainy day that let her talk with Tyler alone. They stayed in his office several minutes after he returned Susan's phone call, and he held Kate and kissed her.

"The more I know about you, the more I want to know," Tyler said. "We need to spend lots of time together so you can answer all my questions."

"And I can learn more about you and what you do," Kate said. "For instance, tonight? You mentioned something about working your shift?"

"Ah. How would you like to help me at the Little Theater? They need more volunteers, and Susan's idea was that board members would work tonight's play and gain exposure. I'm filling in for my grandmother. Susan had thought she and I would work the concession stand together, but I told her Monday night to get someone else. She couldn't find anyone else, so I told her to work the early shift and I'd work the late one. Want to serve flavored waters?"

"Sure. That'd be fun," Kate agreed. Just being with him set her heart pounding.

The rest of Saturday they played Scrabble with Joel and Chelsea, ordered in Chinese for lunch, watched a movie in the huge comfortable chairs in front of the big screen TV, and after the rain quit later that evening, cooked steaks on the big grill in Tyler's backyard. They laughed and teased each other and gazed longingly into each other's eyes.

As soon as dinner was over, Tyler took Kate home. Even serving refreshments at the theater required more than sailing gear. He left her for an hour, then returned in more formal wear. During intermission, the two of them worked behind the high bar in the theater lobby, dispensing sophisticated peach- and raspberry-flavored bottled water.

Sunday morning, Tyler picked her up for church. She sat in the Sinclair pew with his mother and knew the speculative looks from the congregation were warranted this time. There was something between Tyler and her. She wasn't sure what exactly it was or where it would ultimately lead, but it was there, a tangible excitement, a feeling of goodwill and charity toward all.

The minister talked of the spring rain and new beginnings. "Banish anxiety from your heart and cast off the troubles of your body," he quoted from Ecclesiastes, and Kate felt light-hearted and took a deep breath. She looked over at Tyler, who smiled back at her.

Mrs. Sinclair had been kind to her that morning, asked Kate to call her Alma, and told her they expected her for dinner. Kate looked forward to it, not just to learn more about Tyler and the place where he grew up, but to meet Sylvia Sinclair.

"Will your grandmother be joining us for dinner?" she asked as Tyler drove them to the Sinclair house on the hill.

"Yes. She's doing much better. Not quite her normal self, but she'll get there. She's a stubborn old gal, and when she sets her mind to something, she does it. She's determined to get back to her old life, and she will."

Kate looked out the window as Tyler turned on the road that wound up the tallest hill on the outskirts of Bend. She had driven out here once, curious about what the Sinclair home looked like and also to get a view of the McFee house.

"Slow down, please," she said. "That's where the McFees lived." She pointed to a ranch type home that sat much lower than the Sinclair house, another quarter mile up the road. She wondered if his grandmother had run down here or had driven the night of the murder. "Did I tell you that we found Mrs. McFee?"

"You found her?" Tyler asked. "What did she say?"

"Rocky, the retired detective who's working with me on this story, and I went to Illinois Thursday morning, but she was gone. A neighbor told us she'll be back on Monday, so we're going over Tuesday morning."

Tyler pulled the car under the portico, then turned toward Kate. A frown line creased between his eyes. "Would you not mention Mrs. McFee to Grandmother? It upsets her for some reason. I saw fear in her eyes the day I asked her about her old neighbor."

Kate searched her memory and realized she'd never told Tyler what she'd dug up on Loren McFee or that his grandmother was the first one on the scene. "No, I won't bring it up," she promised but vowed to tell him what she knew when he took her home. Right now she wanted to concentrate on this wonderful home and his family.

The entrance hall was lined with portraits. "Tell me who these are," she asked.

Tyler pointed out his great-grandfather, his grandfather and grandmother, his mother and father, and his brother.

"And you," Kate said. The likeness was very good. The strong jaw line, the steel gray eyes that could stare down an adversary or soften to a warm gray when he looked at her as he was now. "This is recent."

"Painted after I took over the company."

"Did you sit for it or was it from a photograph?" Somehow she knew he couldn't sit long enough for a portrait. It was one more thing she was learning about him. He was decisive, which worked well in his job, and he was not one to sit still. She had never seen him sit quietly except in church. Even

when he was driving, he was either waving a hand to empha-
size something he'd said or glancing to the left or right. No,
only when he was communing with the Lord did he remain
serene and still. Another interesting tidbit to add to her internal
file on Tyler Sinclair.

"Photograph," he said. "This way." He led her into a large
living room. A huge rock fireplace dominated the room with
a sitting area in front of it. Mrs. Sinclair and his grandmother
were sitting in wing chairs. Tyler introduced Sylvia Sinclair,
and Kate held out her hand. His grandmother's grip was firm,
which surprised Kate. She thought she would be weaker,
since it hadn't been quite a month since her stroke.

The elder Mrs. Sinclair looked Kate over and nodded when
she had finished her assessment. "You're a good newscaster,"
she said.

"Thank you, Mrs. Sinclair. Your grandson is making some
big changes at the station. I think they'll make WKYS
stronger, and we'll gain more of the market share."

"He's good, like his grandfather. Stubborn, but does right,
and is always working." Her speech wasn't quite clear, each
word not exactly distinct, but Kate could understand her.

Sunday dinner was served in the dining room. A maid
brought in different courses, starting with a crisp spinach
salad and ending with strawberry shortcake. Kate couldn't
help but contrast this Sunday dinner with the one she had
shared with Tyler at the Fullmers'. She almost asked Tyler if
he had heard from Jacob about Woody but didn't want to
bring up anything that would remind Mrs. Sinclair of the dog
story on the night she'd had the stroke.

Instead, with Kate's prompting, Alma was more than happy
to tell childhood stories about Tyler, and Kate chuckled at
every one of them—from the tree house that had collapsed to
the summer trip to Europe when Tyler had been ten and taken
off on his own to explore Rome.

"You have to understand, we'd already been to the Coliseum. I wanted to go back, but the others didn't. I merely decided to do it on my own."

"Yes, but he didn't have much money with him, and he couldn't pay the cab driver for the return trip," Alma said. "I was frantic by that time, but at least he called and explained the problem. So we rescued him."

"Isn't 'rescued' a bit much?" Tyler said. "My plan B was to walk the five miles."

His grandmother laughed. "And he would have done it, too. Tyler can always figure a way out of a problem."

"I think he must take after you," Kate said with a smile, and the old woman gave her a curious stare. "From what Tyler's told me about you, you're a problem solver," she explained. "You look at options and decide the best solution. Like asking Tyler to come back and run the corporation." Last night Tyler had told her about his service career and his goals and his decision to return to Bend.

"The corporation needed him. My husband built it up, and I wanted Tyler to keep it strong," Sylvia Sinclair said and looked at Tyler as if needing affirmation that her decision had been a good one.

"And he's doing a wonderful job," Alma said quickly. "How was the play last night?" She expertly changed the subject, and Kate wondered if his grandmother was having second thoughts about asking Tyler to give up his military career.

They moved back to the large living room, and after coffee, Tyler helped his grandmother back to her room. She protested that she was capable of getting to her room with only her cane for assistance, but Kate noted that once Tyler took Sylvia's arm, she leaned heavily on him.

"Is she doing all right?" Kate asked.

"Better than can be expected," Alma said. "I. . .I feel I owe you an apology for our rocky start at the hospital. I should never have implied that a news story could cause a stroke."

"No apology needed. You were under a lot of pressure, and you were worried about her. That's perfectly understandable." Kate didn't say that the news story on McFee might have elevated Sylvia's blood pressure to the surging point that would send a blood clot to her brain. She didn't know that for a fact, so she kept quiet.

Later when Tyler took her home, she asked him in for coffee and told him all she had discovered about the McFee case.

"Are you saying my grandmother could be involved in a murder?" he asked.

"I don't know what her involvement was. That's what I'm trying to discover."

"For what reason?" He stood and paced over to the front window and stared out. "What good can come of this?"

Kate explained once again about the series for sweeps month and touched on the more recent murders she was also covering. "Do you object to the series?"

"No. Only to involving my grandmother."

"I think your grandmother has been living in fear for forty years. I imagine she'd like the truth to come out."

"What if it causes her another attack? Another stroke, more severe this time? You know how she shuns publicity."

"Now that she's on medication, I doubt that would happen. Besides, I imagine this murder is the reason why she doesn't like publicity. Quotes from her about the murder scene filled the newspaper."

Tyler paced back to the couch, then faced her. "I don't want you to pursue this, Kate."

"What?"

"Focus on the other unsolved murders, not one that's ancient history. Leave my grandmother out of it."

Kate couldn't believe her ears. She remembered when they had met in Shorty's barbecue place after the dog story had aired and she had accused him of censoring the news. He was doing it again.

"If I don't pursue it, Rocky will do it on his own."

"Call him off, too. I don't want this on the news, and I don't want my grandmother upset."

"Tyler," Kate said in her most reasonable voice. "You can't censor the news. We are talking about a crime here. Murder. We need to know the truth. Your grandmother is an old woman who needs peace in her life. Let her find it. This must be resolved."

He sat down hard on the couch and put his head in his hands. He was silent for several tense minutes, then lifted his head. "I don't want my family hurt."

"I don't want to hurt your family," Kate responded. "If your grandmother is innocent, that will come out. But I don't want you to trample on the First Amendment. Are we at an impasse here?"

He stood and once again walked to the front window and back. "No, we're at a place of compromise. Let's find out the facts and evaluate the damage the truth can do or the good it can do. Then we'll make an educated decision."

"All right. I'll talk with Mrs. McFee on my own time Tuesday morning. I know I'm right about Rocky pursuing it without me. He won't drop this. It will be better if I'm there."

"Promise me you won't talk to my grandmother without me. If there's a reason she has to be involved in this, I want to be the one to tell her."

"I promise," Kate said with tears in her eyes. "I'm sorry, Tyler. I'm not trying to destroy your grandmother."

He took her in his arms. "I know. Let's get more facts, then we'll talk again." He kissed her once, then left.

He'd said they weren't at an impasse, but were they? Kate wondered. If she found that his grandmother was involved, would he order her not to pursue it any further? He said that they were at a place of compromise, but Kate feared a compromise might not be possible. And deep down, she sensed that Tyler had the same feeling.

"Dear God, please show me the way." She prayed about it over and over that long evening. Was this what being a broadcaster was all about? Was she tough enough to hound people to get at the truth? She thought about the national news shows she'd seen where ruthless reporters faced down businessmen who had set up bogus corporations as tax dodges or doctors who were cheating on Medicare. She thought of the news anchors who were sent out on location to cover natural disasters and executions of criminals. Was that what climbing the ladder of success meant?

If so, then she wanted to go no further in this news business.

By the time she reported for work on Monday, her head was still throbbing with her inner debate about what she wanted out of life. She'd gone over and over Tyler's stand. After she'd cooled down from her outrage at the possibility of being censored, she had to admit that she'd be as adamant as he if it were her grandmother who was involved. If only tomorrow would come quickly so she could get this thing resolved.

Kate's work on Monday reminded her of the good in her business. That afternoon she covered the story of the quints being released from the hospital. She wouldn't be able to do a live report, since the timing was wrong, but she'd make a tape that would be used the next morning on the network show.

The hospital scene went well. Even though all the babies didn't weigh the magic four pounds, the doctor let the family go home together. Ginger would relax more in her own home, and she had a schedule of volunteers from her church who would be helping with the babies' baths and feedings.

The tape would air on the six o'clock and with a little different view on the ten o'clock. And it was sent via satellite to the network. Kate felt good about getting it finished, so she turned her attention to wrapping up the murder series on Tuesday. Besides the interview with Mrs. McFee, she'd get the final interviews on the other murders. Then she would put that whole series out of her life.

As she was making a few notes on another story, Chelsea plopped down in the chair next to her desk.

"What did you do to Tyler?"

Kate raised her eyebrows.

"Joel says he's as upset as he's seen him in years. What did you do?"

"Why do you think I did something?"

"It's reasonable. You two were two peas in a pod on Saturday. He was as calm and relaxed as I've ever seen him. Then today he's a bear, according to Joel. He called to play racquetball tonight, and Tyler about bit his head off. Said he could use some physical action, and Joel's afraid Tyler will really clobber him tonight."

"We've had a difference in opinion. I really can't talk about it now." Kate blinked hard. Of all times for tears to well up in her eyes. This was not a crying matter. This was her job. When it was over, she might have to leave Bend. Leave Tyler. She couldn't hurt his family and stay in Bend. She didn't know what she would do.

"Well, if you want to talk, I'm here," Chelsea said and walked back to her desk.

Kate turned back to her work but had a hard time concentrating. She knew her relationship with Tyler was at a turning point. Although she had hoped he would, Tyler didn't call that evening. There really was nothing to say until this matter was settled.

She went home after the late news and gave a futile look at her answering machine. No messages. For a second straight night, sleep refused to come, and instead Kate prayed that God would show her the direction her life should take.

৯

The next morning, Kate set her VCR to record her quint story on the network news, then took off for the station, where Rocky was waiting for her. Instead of taking a station car, Kate opted to drive her own. This was her time and her investigation. Tyler didn't want her doing this, so she'd use nothing that belonged to the station. When they arrived at Jane McFee's home, the woman was there.

Jane McFee Horance Lauderback was a small woman. Kate's first impression was that this woman couldn't hurt a fly. Of course, she was forty years older than she'd been when her first husband had been killed, and time had surely changed her.

She met them at the door with a smile on her face. "May I help you?"

Before Kate could answer, Jane McFee grabbed the door frame for support and looked like she would collapse. "Lieutenant Rockwood," she gasped. "I knew you would come back some day."

"Are you all right?" Kate asked and reached out to support the woman.

"No. I'm not all right." She turned to go inside, and Kate held onto her arm and helped her to a couch.

"Is your husband here?"

"No. He's getting a haircut."

"Could I get you some water?" Kate asked, but she didn't wait for an answer. She walked into the kitchen and opened the logical cabinet by the sink for a glass. Rocky was talking to Mrs. McFee when Kate returned with a glass of water.

Mrs. McFee took one sip and then another.

"We want to talk to you about Loren's murder," Rocky said. "We've narrowed the suspects to you and Sylvia Sinclair. You want to tell us what happened that night?"

"I want to see Sylvia," Jane said. "Then I will talk to you."

Kate glanced at Rocky, and his facial expression told her to play along.

"You want to ride with us?" he asked.

"Fine. But first I must call my husband." She looked up the number and dialed. When her husband was called to the phone, her voice held a different tone, not the defeated one that she'd been using, but a more cheerful voice. "An old friend in Bend needs my help, dear, and she's sent a mutual friend to take me there. I'll be back later this afternoon."

"She must think I'm still on the force," Rocky said to Kate in an undertone. "I say we go with it. I'll drive her back myself."

"I don't know. We shouldn't be dishonest."

"Dishonest! We're about to solve a murder case. Let's just go with it."

Kate helped Mrs. McFee into the back seat of her car and drove back to the interstate highway. When they were about fifteen minutes out of Bend, she called Tyler on her cell phone. She gave the operator her name, was switched to Tyler's secretary's office, then Tyler himself came on the line.

"Mrs. McFee and Rocky and I will be at your mother's house in a few minutes. Mrs. McFee wants to talk to your grandmother before she talks to us about that night."

"I'm on my way," he said. "Don't say a word to Grandmother until I get there."

A few minutes later, Kate turned the car up Hill Road. Mrs. McFee had said nothing more on the long trip, but Kate glanced in her rearview mirror when she passed the old McFee home and saw the older woman shiver.

"Why, Kate, this is a surprise," Alma Sinclair said when the maid who let them in took the odd group into the living room. Alma glanced at Jane, back at Kate, then back to Jane again. "Mrs. McFee?"

Not a full minute later Tyler and another man Kate assumed was a lawyer strode into the living room.

"Kate." Tyler acknowledged her presence with a nod and introductions took place. She was right about the lawyer.

"Mrs. McFee, you don't have to tell these people anything," Tyler said.

Mrs. McFee broke her silence. "I want to. I want it finished. I'm an old woman, and I want it ended. I've made peace with my Maker, and now I want to make peace with this world. But first I want to talk to Sylvia."

"In private?" Tyler asked.

"Just tell her I'm here. I have no more secrets."

Tyler left and was gone about five minutes before he returned with Sylvia Sinclair holding onto his arm. Mrs. McFee stood. The older women sized each other up and then embraced.

"It's time," Mrs. McFee said. "I'm ready. Do you have it?"

Mrs. Sinclair sat down heavily on the couch, and Mrs. McFee sat beside her. "Here," Mrs. Sinclair said and handed a handkerchief to her old neighbor.

Mrs. McFee spread the handkerchief on her lap and held up a diamond brooch.

"I knew it wasn't robbery," Rocky said. "And I knew you did it, because you're left-handed. What we want are the details."

"I shot him," Mrs. McFee said.

"In self-defense," Mrs. Sinclair quickly added.

"Oh, yes. He would have killed me," Jane McFee said.

"He nearly had several times before," Mrs. Sinclair said in a steady voice. "He was a brutal man, and he abused Jane time and again. I wasn't surprised that he pulled a gun on her, but I was surprised that she got it away from him and used it on him."

"When did you get there?" Rocky asked. "The telephone

records substantiated Mrs. McFee's story that she called the police before she called you."

Mrs. Sinclair took a deep breath. "Jane ran all the way up here. She was hysterical, and I drove her back down in my car to look the situation over. I decided to cover up the crime."

"No, Sylvia," Mrs. McFee said in an agitated voice. "I couldn't have stood it; you did it for me. My second husband also abused me, but I got out of that marriage quickly. This husband is kind, but I've never told him about Loren."

"Jane, it's time for the whole story to come out. I'm tired of the secret and the deception." Mrs. Sinclair turned toward Rocky. "We messed up the place to make it look like burglary. Once everything was set, I took the brooch and drove home and hid it. Jane called the police, then she called me. I went right down, and we acted like that was the first time I'd been there. We didn't do that for the phone records, but for the timing. I didn't know then that you could check phone records."

"It's what saved you from prosecution," Rocky said to Mrs. McFee. "It fit so well into your story, and when we searched the place and couldn't find the brooch, we didn't think that it could already be moved anywhere else, certainly not to Mrs. Sinclair's home."

"I've been guilt-ridden ever since that day," Mrs. Sinclair said. "Many times I've thought it would have been better if we'd told the truth and let it go to trial, but who would have believed the famous author beat up his wife?"

"I couldn't have stood it then," Mrs. McFee said, "but I feel ten pounds lighter now. Forgive me, Sylvia, for dragging you into this." She held out her hand to Mrs. Sinclair, who took it in both of hers.

"Jane, I wanted to help. I just didn't know what else to do. We've been living a lie for a long time. It does feel good to be free." She glanced at Rocky. "Or are we free? There'll be a trial now, won't there?"

"I don't know. Let me make a couple calls," Rocky said.

He and the lawyer conferred, and then Rocky called the district attorney.

"There's no statute of limitation on murder," Rocky said. "But the D.A. thinks this case should be changed to self-defense. He doesn't have enough to make it murder, so he won't bring charges."

Mrs. McFee slumped in relief. Mrs. Sinclair wiped tears from her face.

"Then it's really over," Mrs. McFee said.

"It's over," Mrs. Sinclair said.

Tyler motioned for Kate to join him, and he escorted her to the entrance hall.

"What now?" he asked once they were out of hearing of the rest. "What are you going to do with this information?"

"I'm doing a series on unsolved murders, but this one is a self-defense shooting. It doesn't fit in," she said.

"Thank you," he said and took her in his arms. "I'm sorry I was so short with you on Sunday. I didn't try to see your side of the issue."

"I wasn't very understanding, either," Kate admitted and looked up into his eyes. "You were trying to protect your grandmother from harm. I was trying to protect freedom of speech, and I lost some perspective. I prayed and prayed about it until I understood more of what you were feeling."

"We worked through this, Kate, just like we'll work through any other problem that comes between us in the next fifty years."

"Fifty years?" Was he implying what she thought?

"At least fifty years, but we'll have to work at it. We should both be less rigid. Compromise a little better. Bend more."

"Bend?" Kate asked. "As in Bend, Kentucky?" In that moment, she knew this was the man for her. And this was the place for her, too. Here in Bend in Tyler's arms.

# *A Letter To Our Readers*

Dear Reader:

In order that we might better contribute to your reading enjoyment, we would appreciate your taking a few minutes to respond to the following questions. When completed, please return to the following:

Rebecca Germany, Managing Editor
Heartsong Presents
PO Box 719
Uhrichsville, Ohio 44683

1. Did you enjoy reading *A Sense of Place?*
   - ❑ Very much. I would like to see more books by this author!
   - ❑ Moderately
     I would have enjoyed it more if _____
     _____

2. Are you a member of **Heartsong Presents**? ❑ Yes ❑ No
   If no, where did you purchase this book? _____
   _____

3. What influenced your decision to purchase this book? (Check those that apply.)

   | | |
   |---|---|
   | ❑ Cover | ❑ Back cover copy |
   | ❑ Title | ❑ Friends |
   | ❑ Publicity | ❑ Other_____ |

4. How would you rate, on a scale from 1 (poor) to 5 (superior), the cover design? _____

5. On a scale from 1 (poor) to 10 (superior), please rate the following elements.

___Heroine     ___Plot

___Hero     ___Inspirational theme

___Setting     ___Secondary characters

6. What settings would you like to see covered in **Heartsong Presents** books?_____

_____

_____

7. What are some inspirational themes you would like to see treated in future books?_____

_____

_____

8. Would you be interested in reading other **Heartsong Presents** titles?    ❏ Yes      ❏ No

9. Please check your age range:
   ❏ Under 18     ❏ 18-24     ❏ 25-34
   ❏ 35-45     ❏ 46-55     ❏ Over 55

10. How many hours per week do you read? _____

Name _____

Occupation _____

Address _____

City_____ State_____ Zip_____

# ·····Hearts♥ng·····

## HEARTSONG PRESENTS *TITLES AVAILABLE NOW:*

# ········ Presents ········

## Great Inspirational Romance at a Great Price!

**Heartsong Presents** books are inspirational romances in contemporary and historical settings, designed to give you an enjoyable, spirit-lifting reading experience. You can choose wonderfully written titles from some of today's best authors like Veda Boyd Jones, Yvonne Lehman, Tracie Peterson, Nancy N. Rue, and many others.

*When ordering quantities less than twelve, above titles are $2.95 each.*
*Not all titles may be available at time of order.*

# Hearts♥ng Presents
# *Love Stories Are Rated G!*

That's for godly, gratifying, and of course, great! If you love a thrilling love story, but don't appreciate the sordidness of some popular paperback romances, **Heartsong Presents** is for you. In fact, **Heartsong Presents** is the *only inspirational romance book club*, the only one featuring love stories where Christian faith is the primary ingredient in a marriage relationship.

Sign up today to receive your first set of four, never before published Christian romances. Send no money now; you will receive a bill with the first shipment. You may cancel at any time without obligation, and if you aren't completely satisfied with any selection, you may return the books for an immediate refund!

Imagine. . .four new romances every four weeks—two historical, two contemporary—with men and women like you who long to meet the one God has chosen as the love of their lives. . .all for the low price of $9.97 postpaid.

*To join, simply complete the coupon below and mail to the address provided.* **Heartsong Presents** romances are rated G for another reason: They'll arrive *Godspeed!*